Triangle Ray

Stories

John Holman

DZANC
BOOKS

DZANC BOOKS

5220 Dexter Ann Arbor Rd.
Ann Arbor, MI 48103
www.dzancbooks.org

Library of Congress Cataloging-in-Publication Data

Holman, John, 1951-
  [Short stories. Selections]
  Triangle Ray : stories / John Holman. -- First edition.
    pages ; cm
  ISBN 978-1-938103-37-7
  I. Title.
  PS3558.O35593A6 2016
  813'.54--dc23

                                    2015022767

First US edition: January 2016
ISBN: 978-1-938103-37-7
Book design by Michelle Dotter

This is a work of fiction. Characters and names appearing in this work are a product of the author's imagination, and any similarity to real persons, living or dead, is coincidental and not intended by the author.

Printed in the United States of America

10   9   8   7   6   5   4   3   2   1

Contents

For Rick.

Sunday

IMAGINE RAY AT SEVENTEEN, HIS SENIOR YEAR, LATE SEPTEMBER, studious. It's 1979, and Marie Hargrove has come back to school after missing all of last year and most of the previous one because of illness. Rumor was that she almost died, and Ray has learned that it's true. She was sick a long time before doctors saw she had cancer. She had the surgery, ovaries removed, but then something else happened, another organ threatened, and she endured radiation and chemotherapy. Amazing, Ray thinks.

She is healthy now, knock on wood, and she knocks on Ray's forehead in the media center where they meet during lunch hour for study, talk, stifled laughs.

Marie's class graduated two years ago, the year she first got sick. Now here she is, twenty at her next birthday, a grown woman among the girls and boys. She could be a teacher, Ray tells her, as sophisticated as she seems. She's gorgeous really, dresses elegantly compared to everybody else—not as trendy as most of the other girls, and not as dowdy as most of the teachers. She wears crisp, thin-striped blouses and straight summer wool skirts, has smooth brown skin and short, silky black hair. Sometimes, when she wears her hair loose, and maybe some lipstick, a thin gold necklace quietly radiant against her skin, she looks too wonderful, like she could be on the covers of the fashion magazines in the media center. She says she intends to be a doctor.

They don't plan the meetings at lunchtime. Ray and Marie just happen to be there while other kids are smoking in the parking lot or sneaking off campus to drink vodka, to look at porn, to shoplift the 7-11, and speeding back to school by 1:30 for class. Wild and rowdy. Ray has done some of that, last year. But now the media center envelops him, shuts all that out. He doesn't want any trouble that would jeopardize his going to college. And he wants to prove to himself that he can make A's for once. All A's. Marie studies a textbook, French or history, something heavy with a crackling spine and slick, densely printed pages; Ray reads magazines, having studied nearly all he plans to at home. He likes *Esquire* and the newsweeklies, *Psychology Today* and *The New Yorker* cartoons, *Mademoiselle* and *Vogue*. He likes the beautiful women in the good clothes, the poses, the coolness, the skin, something bright in the models' clear eyes. Marie says it's the airbrushing that makes them amazing, and light—the light the photographer shines on them; it's external and artifice, she says. That's all right, Ray says. Anyway, he thinks, who airbrushed you?

They flirt. That's what Mrs. Holiday, the media center director, calls it. Pretending he doesn't know what she means, Ray keeps his angular face serious. His smile, the unconscious one, is open and generous—innocent despite the faint, never shaved but trimmed and monitored mustache, the dark fuzz on his chin, the new sideburns his barber smoothes out with clippers after shaping his moderate 'fro. Shining eyes. Six-three. In the media center he can avoid the basketball coach, a gray-haired stick man who is ever pressing Ray to try out for the team. Ray doesn't even like basketball, although he'll play on the outdoor court sometimes with friends after school. He's embarrassed to be tall and not like it. He'd rather read. He likes football but his mother won't let him play, afraid her gangly son will be broken. His father says, "Run track." So Ray runs track. Runs distance—mile and cross-country. Here's the thing about basketball: while the other guys are dreaming about making the winning shot, the crowd going wild, Ray dreams about missing it. He actually dreams about it. He'd just as soon skip that possible reality.

He has a smile for Marie that's calculated, practiced. His eyes thin and his chin lifts. Rakish, Mrs. Holiday says to him one day. It is a smile for posing as splendid, for assuming a worldliness to put against Marie's maturity, her serenity, her experiences that astound him to imagine. Over her book, she watches him. She tilts her head to the side, arches an eyebrow, smiles with the tip of her tongue between her teeth. Mrs. Holiday gives them a similar look from behind the checkout counter, as if they are too cute for words, as if she hopes they know what they're in for.

Sometimes he thinks Mrs. Holiday is flirting with him. The idea makes him bolder with Marie, whom he more or less thinks of as an older woman. Marie is the first girl to really interest him and show it back to him face to face, who has triggered his wit and answered it, who has sat still and allowed him the wish to touch her face, kiss her neck, pull her to him by the waist. Some days he can see Marie's bra through her blouse. Her body is thin and full at once. Her face has a glow. He can say things that make her close her French book and laugh convulsively, quietly, and hard, her teeth strong and white, tears brightening her eyes, her head ducked low over the shiny media center table. Making her laugh makes his day.

One Friday she agrees he can probably visit her at home after church. Next Sunday. He's been asking to see her, hoping for greater privacy than this big, sparsely used room. "Since you don't go to football games, and you won't go to a movie with me, the least you could do is let me come visit you."

"Ray, it's not that I don't and I won't. I have choir practice, there's the volunteer stuff at the hospital, and our youth group has to work on Fridays at the rescue mission. I don't have time for much else. I have to study sometime, kid. Pre-med, then med school, right? Gotta get it done." Sometimes, talking to him, she gets passionate about amino acids.

She slides his English notebook over to her side of the table and writes down her phone number. He pulls it back and looks at it, eights and sixes and fives written in fuchsia ink, bright and voluptuous. He's never seen sexier numbers.

"These are the most alluring digits I've ever witnessed," he says, affecting a British accent. "What's your address?"

She smiles and pauses. Then she tells him. An address on Monty Street. He writes it down and shows it to her. "Look at your writing and look at mine. I make a scrawl like the tracks of a panicked snake."

She laughs and slams shut the notebook. "I'm surprised you got out of third grade."

He makes a serious face, pretending to be offended. "Monty Street?" he says. "Never heard of it."

She laughs again. "You ought to come to my church. It's first Sunday and my choir is singing."

"Thanks. Maybe. But Sunday sometime for sure."

"You have my numbers, then."

"Indeed."

When Sunday comes, he doesn't have a car. They didn't set a definite time, either, but he figures church for her is over by one—no later. He didn't think to actually call her Saturday—well, he did think about it, but Saturday just leaked away while he was basking in the memory of Friday and looking forward to Sunday. He had no interest in going to her church. He stopped going to his parents' church a couple of years ago, shortly after he joined it and was baptized but not before he tired of trying to understand its appeal to others. He thought the preaching was too theatrical. There was something interesting about the baptism, though—an all-new wooziness when the minister raised him from the water of the church's white baptismal behind the pulpit. Wet, he waited for insight. He felt expectant, dazed, ambiguous. By the time he was dry and in the car with his parents, he wondered what exactly he had felt. Was it lightheadedness, or was it the lightness of being unburdened? Unburdened of what? There was a residue of wonder the next day, but by dinnertime and homework it was gone. A memory, or a tease—fleeting and frustrating.

"You're old enough to explore for yourself," his mother said when he decided to take a break from Sunday sermons. She cited Jesus's seeking, and Siddhartha's, his mother the English teacher at the junior college. And he's read *Siddhartha*. It shames him slightly that he is neither of those spiritually adventurous men, that his own skepticism is rooted in ignorance rather than courage. He would welcome some wisdom. All he can do is stare at the stars and ask the night air for meaning, then go back in the house and watch TV. He has stood out there and asked the starry air about Marie, the sky sparkling and fathomless, staring back.

Sunday his father is out of town in Virginia at a funeral for a cousin Ray has never seen. His father's cousin. His mother is going to church, and then to a dinner for the minister. She invites Ray, but of course Ray says no. He has a study date, he says. With Marie Hargrove, over on the east side.

"And how are you going to get there?"

He'd thought maybe his friend Handy could give him a ride, although he hasn't asked Handy, and Handy is probably going to church himself, and he doesn't really want Handy to know what he's up to with Marie. All he's said to Handy is, "Where's Monty Street?"

He doesn't tell his mother all of that. He says, "I'd hoped to drive myself, before Dad had to leave."

"Yes, but I need my car today, Ray-Ray. And how is Marie Hargrove?"

"She's fine. You know her?"

"I know who she is. I kind of know her parents. She was a sick girl for a while."

"You know she's back in school? We have a couple of classes together."

"Yes. I figured. The study date, right? You could take the bus, I guess."

"Right."

"Tell her and her folks hello for me. And be careful in that part of town."

Ray thinks, of course his mother probably was aware of the pretty girl with cancer at his school. But before this year *he* hadn't thought much about Marie. When he'd come to the high school in ninth grade she'd been one in the flood of older kids he did not know, but she stood out early in a school play as the shotgun-wielding old lady defending her property against developers. People praised her performance. After that, she was gone. Ill, people said. Really ill. Pregnant, a few guessed. Cancer, somebody else said. And that last was unimaginable. Ray forgot about her. It's incredible, he thinks, that he might never have known her. That she might have died. Almost as startling is that she even existed before now.

He leaves just after his mother does. He walks two blocks away from his street to a bus stop and waits twenty minutes. Cars go by, nobody he knows. He has no idea what bus will take him to Marie's neighborhood. The bus driver, when he arrives, explains the transfer and takes him south to town, where he waits another long time for the right bus. Then he isn't sure where to get off. That driver is no help, lets him off at a big commercial intersection. "You're close," the driver says. "I don't go down that street."

As the noise of the departing bus fades away, grit and exhaust settling in its wake, Ray thinks, "I have no visible means of support," which means he doesn't know what to do now and there is no one to guide him. The thought tickles him. Even as he stands on the littered street corner, concrete solidly under his feet, he envisions himself floating there, hovering, buoyed by affection for Marie. Perhaps this is faith, he thinks, envisioning Marie's happy face if he could craft the joke for her. Gazing at the Eckerd's across the street, Ray realizes that he has always had faith of a sort, and he realizes that he will soon need a plan. There will come a time when he can no longer gamble on the world's benevolence, when his adventures could render crippling results. He's thinking of when he has taken tests without studying, chancing that the questions will be the ones he can answer; of the racing he and some boys have done with their parents' cars, taking curves fast; of swallowing some pill supplied by somebody's brother or cousin; of roaming with bored kids through the high school gym parking lot during a basketball game and stealing car batteries from unlocked cars, then stacking them in a pyramid on the unused tennis court. He usually has no clue how he could explain his behavior, or what he might do if he crashed or got caught. But now, he can almost see the careful future, can certainly sense it, and it makes this venture out for Marie all the more rousing. It's the last risk, he thinks. If he can cause her to love him before she discovers his fear, his disconnection from what she seems certain of, then he might never be afraid again, he might be grounded then, and all his care will be to protect and keep Marie; and if he fails, he thinks, his heart will be hammered, he would be as crushed as the yellowed cigarette butts at his feet.

Right now, he's too early. It's 11:50. Marie wouldn't be home yet, so no use in calling. Besides, he left her phone number at home, on the same sheet of notebook paper with her address. He's not sure he remembers the phone number, but he remembers the number to look for on her house, the gorgeous numbers.

It is the first Sunday in October, warm again after a cool preview of fall the last few days. In the near-noon sun, Ray's new tan corduroy pants look yellow, as do his brushed and silicone-sprayed desert boots. His long-sleeved knit shirt is brown. When he left the house he thought he looked autumnal—he felt good. Now his shoes look like clown shoes, and he feels too hot, probably looks uncomfortable, too. He lopes across the street. He pulls on Eckerd's locked door, but a few people who work there are moving around inside. He waits in the shade of the awning until a man wearing a necktie and a snug blue shirt unlocks the door at twelve. The man is the manager; his nametag says Joe Tate.

Ray's the only customer. He walks the aisles trying to think of something he needs, a reason to be there. He looks at foot powder, razor blades, hair dye, lawn chairs, laxatives, film, cameras, batteries, electrical tape, reading glasses, vitamins, Epsom salt, shaving cream, cookies, canned nuts, Halloween candy, Halloween costumes and makeup, lipstick, eye shadow, fingernail polish, shoe polish, shoe dye, boxes of tampons and pads. He examines a box of "mini maxi pads." Could he joke with Marie about that later? He'd like to ask her the values of ultra thin maxi, thin ultra, super maxi, regular maxi thins, super ultra and long. He'll pretend only the language interests him, but he will have achieved an intimacy—brought the language to bear on that curly-haired part of her.

He'd like to browse this drug store with her, talk about hair conditioners, hair removers, skin lotions, pumice stones, cotton balls, earwax softeners, deodorants, straight-edged and angled tip tweezers, toothpaste, waxed and unwaxed floss. He imagines living with her among products from these aisles. He imagines looking from her bed to her night table at the Vicks VapoRub there, the vials of pills she might still have to take for maintenance of her health, the LED clock she might have chosen from behind the front counter of this store.

Joe Tate comes up to him at the greeting cards display. "Can I help you find something?" he asks.

"No. Maybe," Ray says. "You got any maps?"

The manager leads Ray past rolls of cellophane-sheathed gift wrap and bright satiny bows to a rack of folded maps and magazine-sized atlases. He spins the rack and leaves Ray standing there, as if his fortune will be revealed when the spinning stops. As the revolving rack slows, Ray can see that his fortune is probably not right in front of him. These are road maps of the Southeastern states, of Texas, of the Midwest and West and Northeast. He needs a map of Durham, to learn how to get to Monty Street.

More people have entered the store. It's 12:18. At the magazine shelves he looks around to see if Joe Tate is watching him. He's afraid he looks suspicious. He picks up a slick photography journal featuring a swimming black-and-white nude on the cover. The picture of the woman in the pool stirs a memory of when he and a group of boys, about three years ago, sneaked into the downtown theater that showed X-rated films. That was an amazingly thrilling day, to have been dropped downtown by somebody's older brother, to sneak through the back door of the theater, to scrunch down in the dark second row and see things on the screen that he couldn't believe someone would let be filmed, let be shown. His body felt thrummed by the images, like a thick vibrating string on a bass violin. He thought, it's no wonder I'm not supposed to be here. It was a black-and-white movie in which a man finds a woman bathing in his tub. Like the woman in the bath water, the woman in the pool is partly submerged, her skin shiny-wet. How, he wonders, can mere images engage him so? How can the memory of one affect him still?

This day is something like that one years ago. He feels almost as thrilled by the hope that Marie, fragrant from church, will maneuver them into a corner of her house for a kiss. He wonders: if his memory can reconstitute that real and thrilling moment in the movie theater, then can his wish for that kiss conjure the future?

The images dissolve as Ray looks up from the photograph to a very old man who stands at the other end of the magazine shelves. A younger woman brushes the man's coat sleeve and leaves him there. He is well dressed in a dark blue suit, white shirt, blue-and-green striped tie, and dark blue hat. His bald head seems scaly under the hat. His nose is as pale as paste, but with tiny purple veins along the nostrils and tip. He stares at the shelves, eyes wet and blue, a clear glistening string of mucus lengthening from his nose. The man doesn't seem to know about his nose leak, or doesn't care, or can't do anything about it. Then he farts, little pops, and the floating stink forces Ray to put down the photography journal and walk away.

It's time to go, maybe, depending on how long it will take him to walk the rest of the way to Marie's house. 12:30, now. He takes a can of Coke from the refrigerated case to the checkout counter, pays for it, and asks the clerk directions to Monty Street. A few blocks, a few turns. The clerk, a woman in a blue Eckerd smock, her right front tooth surrounded by silver, smiles at him. Her hair is shiny black and curled in tight even rolls, as if recently shaped with a curling iron. Something about her reminds him of Mrs. Holiday, the media center director. Maybe her height; she's short. And her playful wink. "Come back and see me," she says. But Mrs. Holiday is much more sophisticated, much more subtle, more like Marie.

Back outside, it takes a while for the warmth to take hold after the air conditioning of the store. Ray drinks the Coke, then crosses the boulevard, walks slowly in the direction the lady told him to go, moves away from the commercial district of Captain D's, McDonald's, gas stations, Discount Daybeds. These are long blocks, but tree-lined after a while. The houses are huge with wide yards but old and rundown. Some of them are boarding houses. A barking dog startles Ray as he walks by a leaning slat fence. He tries not to sweat, succeeds somehow by willing it away, by staying cool, but the dog has caused a prickle under his arms. His scalp itches.

He remembers the old man at the magazines in the store. There was a man who has lived past his time, Ray thinks. Death should be for the old, not for people as young as Marie. He's never known anyone who has died. His grandparents were dead before he was born. But Marie has told him about younger people she has known through her illness who have died. Kids with leukemia, with brain cancer, kids with a hole in the heart. You risk your life just by being born, he thinks. He wonders about his father's cousin. How old was he? His father's age probably, surely not as old as the man in the store. That old man could have been a ghost, as pale as he was.

He reaches Marie's street at the 100 block. Marie's address is 629. The walk starts out level, past duplexes, a brick apartment building with a dirt yard and clothes hanging in open doorways, more small houses painted lime, blue, pink. Two men in white undershirts sit on the stoop of a pink house, flanking a thin woman sitting draped in big clothes—a black T-shirt studded with large, glittering multicolored disks, red shorts as wide as a skirt, and fluffy leopard-print slippers. They pull on her long hair, braiding it. At another house with a tarpapered roof, three men lean under the hood of a rusting white car on the broken concrete driveway. It looks like they are playing with a baby that's sitting on the motor. One of the men turns toward the street and takes out his teeth, which he wraps in a sheet of paper before turning back to the baby under the hood. Ray remembers that his mother told him to be careful. He's being careful, other than that he is a stranger in new preppy clothes in this strange street. He could yell, "Take that baby off that motor, you idiots!" That could be dangerous.

Otherwise, there aren't many people about, driving by, walking by, sitting outside. A quiet Sunday. The street turns downhill and Ray realizes he's been walking uphill. He still resists pushing up his sleeves, wanting to arrive unwrinkled at Marie's. His heartbeat quickens to be nearer to her.

Finally he gets to her house, the address he recalls, a yellow shingle-sided house with a dark brick lip of a porch and flaked green metal chairs against the wall. The screen door is dusty in the glare of the sun, and although the inner door is open he can only see darkness beyond the screen. It's an old-fashioned screen door in a wooden frame and hooked from inside; so maybe someone is home. He knocks. Waits. Puts his face close to the dusty-pale screen, hoping to see dim furniture, a hallway. Something. He peers through dust into darkness. He turns around to look at the sunny street, wondering if he is at the right house. The empty driveway sparkles with bits of broken glass in the pavement. The sun brightens the houses across the street. Next door a metallic-blue truck crowds the curb.

An old purple Javelin rolls down the street and two boys sit up front, elbows out the windows, seeming to swoon from the sound of scratchy guitars and voices roiling out of the radio. The boys look heavy-lidded and stoned. The car rolls away and there's silence again, almost as if it never happened.

Ray knocks and says into the space beyond the screen, "Hello. Is this Marie Hargrove's house?" No one answers, and Ray leans his face closer, his nose touching the wire. Now, seeing nothing in the dark house, he feels a faint itch to sneeze. He could sneeze right into Marie's living room, let his damp breath spread out for her, like a swarm of microscopic fireflies, like tiny fiber optic lights he's read about, like a radiant wind, maybe settle on Marie and cover her, light her body so that he can find her. Then he sneezes through the screen, blowing dust, as a tiny orange light moves in the darkness. He looks again, then he relocates it. It moves up, stops, glows, then moves down. Somebody is smoking a cigarette in there. He sneezes again, this time turning away and covering his mouth with his hand. Somebody is looking out at him. "Hello?" Ray says. "Is Marie home?" The cigarette hovers. He thinks, this must be the wrong house. Then he thinks, somebody could have a gun on me, and he steps back off the porch to the driveway.

Or Marie could be in there watching him with her whole family, waiting for him to go away, whispering, *He actually thought I was serious? He thought I'd be interested in a seventeen-year-old boy?* Ray doesn't know what to do. He imagines her in there with her mother and father and grandparents, cousins too, all singing softly, *Oh, why must he be a teenager in love?* silently cracking up the way Marie does in the media center. He has a slight feeling of dizziness, as if the air around him has just rippled. Feeling his heart thud, he walks to the curb, where he looks back at the house, and then affects an amble up the street. People, maybe people from school, could be watching him from all the houses. When he has passed a few, he jogs until he's climbed the hill, sweating, squinting in the sunlight, feeling foolish and angry. And he cannot direct the anger. He pushes up his sleeves. Why is he so out of breath? He runs all the time.

Why had Marie told him he could come over if she wasn't going to be home, or wasn't going to let him in? Why had he come here without being sure what time he should arrive? Why had he worn these new, heavy clothes? And why was he walking? Why had he run?

He gazes back down the hill and considers going back. Who was in that house looking at him, saying nothing, mocking him? Did he even go to the right house? Could there be more than one street with this name? He looks up at the street sign at the next corner. Sure enough, he's at the intersection of Monty Court and Monty Street. He walks all the way to the cul-de-sac and up the other side in disgust that there isn't a house numbered the same as what Marie told him. He doubts the number he remembers now, the number he wrote down in his English notebook that is in his backpack on his bed at home. The bed on which he has rolled with his pillow and repeated Marie's name like a mantra. Either he's gotten the number wrong or Marie has lied to him.

But maybe Marie will see him walking by her house and step out to wave him in. Maybe she'll come riding by in a station wagon with her family and beckon him to follow the car to the right driveway. But he'd be embarrassed to see her now, having forgotten the house number, wandering like a vagrant, stranded like prey flushed out into the open. And wouldn't her family be having dinner after church? He was certainly not invited to dinner. Marie has set him up, or he was just stupid, letting her make him think somebody as beautiful, smart, and talented as she could really care about him. Or he's here on the wrong Sunday, or she never really *offered* an invitation. He should have called her last night. He can't believe he didn't call. He's never called her. He's been too caught up in the play and romance of the media center, believing in that private magic, not wanting to weaken the intensity of seeing her there by wasting talk on the phone. Fool. Maybe she doesn't exist outside of school. Maybe she's ghost, a dead girl after all.

Then, once again, the houses and yards and cars and trees are images painted on the air, and the air is like a curtain that surrounds him, and the curtain billows. None of this could be real, he thinks. But then he thinks, it's real. Even the unreal is real if it is happening to me. He's still hot. He's still in love with Marie. He still has to get home. And he expects to go to school tomorrow to see Marie in the media center and to find out what has happened here today. He'll just have to wait. He looks around until the air is still again; the images are still, until the deep world returns nearly as it was.

Cannon

THE BOY, SEVEN YEARS OLD, GRIPPED THE CHAINS AND PUMPED his legs until he rode the rubber seat of the swing to the heights of tree limbs. The backswing took him into the shade of the woods behind his house and the forward thrust raised him into the afternoon sunlight of the yard. Pumping, he rode the curve of air like a pendulum. Into the sun he could see his father's head through the kitchen window, fluorescence glinting on his father's scalp. Into the shade he was a bullet in the barrel of a gun ready to fire. Into the sun he saw his father's face look out at him and smile, his father's soapy hand wave. Into the shade he was an intake of breath, then a comet. Into the sun he saw the slope of yard, the grass waving like the wind he rode. Into the shade his back brushed the bark of a pine tree, sunlight slid along the pine needles. Into the sun he saw his father's back which blocked his view of the pots on the kitchen stove, and the ground moved under him like a wave. Into the shade he was a high diver atop a platform. Into the sun he let go of the chains and flipped backward while sailing forward, a cannonball spinning for no other purpose than flight.

When the ground came, it was hard. Pain shot through his arm and shoulder and soaked into his back and skull. He couldn't breathe and that terrified him. Air was in the sky. He wanted desperately to breathe before his father got to him. This pain, this emptiness of air, was a mistake. He didn't want to be helpless. He heard the back door slam, footfalls in the grass. His father's voice, calling "Ray," unusually high-pitched. His father's face was above him. His father's face blocked the sky and air was in his mouth. Sweat slicked his father's forehead. His father's mouth was large and firm. His father's mustache brushed Ray's nose. His father pinched Ray's nostrils and blew air into his mouth. Ray gasped and gulped air. His father turned him on his side and lifted him. Pain shot through his shoulder and swallowed his arm. Tears squeezed from Ray's eyes. He held onto his father's shirt with one hand but not the other. He thought his other arm was still on the ground, but he couldn't see it as his father carried him out of the yard.

That's what I wrote for the continuing education writing class I took. I was twenty-nine, finally dedicated to doing something with my life. I had stories to tell. On the first day of class, we were told to write a true sentence using first person, then to write one using third person. First I wrote, "I didn't make up my bed this morning." The teacher, a very short white-haired woman, nodded, frowned, and said nothing. Then I wrote, "He deliberately wrecked the powder-blue Pinto his father gave him for his birthday." The teacher said, "You seem to tell more significant truths in third person." I nodded, frowned, and said nothing. Then we were told to go home and write about an early frightening event. So I wrote about hurting myself in that fall. I had to revise it about three times before the teacher said to stop. I did it in first person, then in third person; then I added some lyrical touches.

My dad also used to tell the story of when I broke my arm. Dad had mixed or changing motives when he told it, depending on who was listening. Basically, it was to make fun of me, good-naturedly, and I guess I good-naturedly endured it. He would tell it at the bar-ber shop when men were talking loudly about dumbness. He would tell it to my high school friends as a weekend warning for us not to go "cannonballing" all over town, don't get into trouble, you know. Or he would bring it up when he thought I was embarking on some dangerous idea, like the time I wanted to buy a Volkswagen bus that was incredibly cheap because the brakes were bad, the shocks were shot, and the exhaust leaked up through the floor into the cab. That was just before he surprised me with the Pinto, which I did not deliberately wreck. He told it to Marie and her parents the night they came over for dinner to discuss our desire to be married. I was eighteen years old and Marie had just turned twenty-one. We were about to be high school graduates.

In part, I allowed, he was giving them some of our family lore, a gesture to ease them into the family, or to show them what kind of family they would be joining if the wedding were to happen. I thought, too, it was to point out my shortcomings when it came to foresight, a hint that my wish to be married might be poorly considered. Never mind that when I was seven years old I was unlikely to give much forethought to anything other than Halloween and Christmas.

"He believed," Dad explained, "that he could launch from the upswing, flip as many times as he wanted, and land on his feet, I guess." That great plan still tickled Dad, eleven years later. The swing set was made of timber and bolts and chains. It had two swing seats and a seesaw. Dad and his brother, Uncle Lee, had built it for me. An hour before my launch, I had been in my bedroom trying to predict which card would turn up from a deck Dad shuffled. It was one of our after-school games, me trying to make myself special with the discovery that I had ESP. Dad had been telling the Hargroves that, too. "Anyway," he said now, "he might get lucky and guess the two of clubs, but he couldn't predict that he might break his neck or leg or arm if he cannonballed onto hard ground." Ha ha.

We all laughed at my idiocy. It broke—ha!—some of the tension, as neither my parents nor Marie's seemed enthusiastic about our plans. So our laughing together, even at me, was a good sign. My mother seemed happy right then, party-red lipstick brightening her pretty smile. Marie's mother chuckled deeply, her large hoop earrings swinging against her cheeks. Plus, the food was tasty and they were drinking wine. Marie and I were hopeful that if the parents hit it off, we might get their cheerful consent.

Unlike other times Dad told the story, that night he didn't stop at what was funny to him. He told about taking me to hospital, about how frightened he was about my arm. Both forearm bones were broken, the ulna and the radius. "When I held it," he said, "the arm bent in the middle like a cooked noodle." He worried about severed nerves, muscle tear, blood blockage. He couldn't remember the proper first aid, so when he should have made a splint he tried to use a scarf from Mom's drawer for a sling. Maybe the mouth-to-mouth was appropriate, maybe not. I'd knocked the breath out of myself. He stretched me out on the backseat of the car and drove me to the emergency room when he should have called for an ambulance. "I'm telling you," he said, "I cursed stop lights and pot holes and everything responsible for them, including the mayor, the board of aldermen, and the rain. I was mad at Beverly" (Mom) "for being out of town at a conference. Mad at myself for not being out back with Ray instead of in the kitchen trying to get dinner on." Driving, he remembered turning off all the burners on the stovetop, but he couldn't remember turning off the oven. He kept telling me, "We're almost there, we're almost there." If it wasn't for this or that damned traffic light, that damned blocked lane, that damned slowpoke in the exhaust-spewing pickup truck pulling out in front of us, we'd have been there already.

He said, "When I hustled Ray into the emergency room I saw how wrong that silk scarf sling was. The triage nurse gently removed it and had him lie on a gurney, Ray's wobbly little arm across his stomach. I stuffed the scarf into my pocket and debated about when to call Beverly."

While Dad debated, I lay silent in the emergency area hallway and held my throbbing wrist with my good hand. All of the treatment rooms were occupied. Other people waited on gurneys, too. My throat was dry and I couldn't work up enough moisture to swallow. I said I was thirsty, and when Dad snagged a nurse going by she told us I couldn't have anything to eat or drink before a doctor said it was okay. "Why, for God's sake?" Dad asked. "Either get a doctor out here to see him or get him some water, please."

"I'm sorry, sir. Just please be patient."

"Just be patient," he said to me, smiling. "Funny, huh?" He touched my forehead, as if to check for a fever. "Does your arm hurt bad?"

I was slow to answer. "I don't know."

That sent another wave of panic through him. If my arm was numb, maybe it was dead. But when he looked at me I was obviously in pain, and afraid, tears wetting my lashes.

I felt a terrific ache all through me. I didn't know what really hurt and what didn't. I didn't know if the pain was extraordinary or not. I said, "Is my arm going to fall off?"

"No," he said, chuckling. "We're going to get it fixed. You're going to get an X-ray, but that won't hurt."

He still didn't know why I couldn't have anything to drink. It was absurd. There I was, not even complaining, asking only for water, and I couldn't even get that in a hospital. "He needed his mom," Dad said to Marie, who sat next to me, across from her mother and father at the dining table. My parents sat at the ends. I felt as if Marie and I were like a little David couple confronting two sets of Goliaths. Dad's talking about my childhood was undermining my hope to seem a grown-up. It was odd enough that we were eating in the dining room, that I was sharing the table with both my parents at the same time, that the table was set with the good china and heavy silver and gold-rimmed wine and water glasses. "He needed someone more skilled at confrontation, more skilled at comforting him." Tears filled Dad's eyes, now as well as then. He said, "I looked at his little face, at how brave he was being. It hurt me that I couldn't help him. I felt guilty, helpless, like he deserved a better dad."

"You're getting all sentimental, now, Melvin," Mom said.

"Yeah, I know," Dad said.

"Looks to me like you're a great dad," Mr. Hargrove said.

"Anyway, I stopped a different nurse going by and asked for water. 'He didn't get his dinner. He's been playing outside. All he wants is some water.'"

"Hang in there, dude," she said. She must have noticed my teary eyes. "I'll check on something for his thirst."

Dad told us, "I wished I had a deck of cards so that we could play ESP. Ray, you hardly ever guessed a card right. Sometimes you'd stare at the back of a card for minutes before guessing wrong. You would touch it, close your eyes in what looked like painful concentration. You were stubborn. And as prescient as a brick." He looked around at the rest of the table. He said, "I stared at other patients. I wondered what their problems were. If any were life-threatening. But would they still be waiting in the hall if so? Who could say Ray's injury wasn't? A bone sliver in the bloodstream finding the heart or the brain."

The Hargroves, Marie included, wore slight smiles, in sympathy for Dad's fear but aware that it was for nothing. There I was sitting among them, my arm intact.

"Down the hall," he said, "a kid about Ray's age was in a wheelchair, his dark scrawny leg home-bandaged with a blood-stained yellow washcloth and tape. The triage nurse hadn't removed that. His grandmother stood beside him. She kept telling everyone who would listen, 'He got bited by a dog. My little grandboy. I don't know what kind but that dog don't belong to nobody.' She had gray, too-tight cornrows that started near the top of her head. Looked like they ought to hurt. Woven in were red threads. The boy was whimpering. For some reason, that grandma made me mad.

"An old white man was on a gurney on the other side of the hall. He was by himself, a sheet up to his neck, his eyes closed the whole time. I'd stare to see if he was breathing. He had white scruff on his pasty face, and white hair filled his nostrils like cotton batting. He could have been dead."

Marie said, "Healthcare in this country needs a lot of work. Sometimes I think about going into hospital administration after med school."

"One thing at a time," Mr. Hargrove said. "First college. People change their minds a lot in college, sometimes." He looked at her unsmiling, as if waiting for her to change her mind now, about marrying me, I feared. "Anyway, it's the insurance industry that needs an overhaul."

Dad sucked his teeth, a habit that both Mom and I found annoying. He shrugged. "Yeah, I guess." He picked something off his tongue with his napkin. "So this old guy is lying there. People in blue scrubs and funky rubber clogs scurried by pushing blood-pressure carts and carrying clipboards. I got to wondering if some of them were sick, too. If they had deep worries that you couldn't tell just by looking at them."

He said he remembered a time he waited for Mom at the airport when she was returning from a different conference. She had been in Colorado, and, as he said, "Ray was with me at the gate, five then, concentrating hard on a plastic dinosaur he wobbled across the blue seat beside him. People moved to their gates, deplaned, their faces searching, happy with reunion or blank. And then, coming off the plane your mama was on—do you remember this, Ray?—was a woman with torrential tears, helped along through the crowds by another woman."

I knew that story, all right. I didn't remember it happening, but Dad had told it enough times I knew the moral he drew from it. "Dad," I said, "how about a more cheerful subject."

Mr. Hargrove looked like he was ready for a smoke break. He was fiddling with a pack of matches on the table in the space where his dinner plate had been, since Mom and I had cleared the table of everything but dessert plates and forks and glasses. Mr. Hargrove nodded patiently and said, "Let's hear it, Mel. I'll bet we can take it."

"The one crying," Dad said, "was so distraught that no amount of public scrutiny could stop her. Her face was awful, twisted, lifted to the ceiling, emitting deep heart-wrenching grunts. She had on some kind of orange fur coat. Beverly came through the jetway door looking grim. Everybody looked grim. They had traveled hours on that plane with that woman. Her husband had died during their vacation, see—suffocated from an allergic reaction to eating shrimp. Her sister, the lady who helped her along, had flown to Denver to fetch her."

Mom said, "Weeping and wailing had come from their row near the middle of the plane for the whole otherworldly flight. It was horrible. Poor thing." She drew in her lips, dimples appearing in her thin cheeks.

Dad said, "You expect misery in a hospital, but who can tell, other places, who is hurting, what dreaded mission someone is on, what suffering goes on in public? We don't always see it."

"You're so right," Mr. Hargrove said.

"Anyway," Dad said, "in the hospital, I massaged Ray's little legs to distract him from his arm. I didn't want to wait any longer to call Beverly, but I didn't want to leave him to find a phone. Then I thought, why worry her with incomplete news? She was in Miami this time, probably not in the hotel anyway. I hoped she wouldn't have to endure another grim flight, this time with her own grief, maybe coming home to a boy who would have his arm amputated or something."

Dad had put me in a glum mood. Yet it seemed to charm Marie and the mothers. This dinner was supposed to be about my future with Marie. And what was Dad doing? Talking about pain and misery, basically being a downer.

I said, "Dad, do you think there are places where people are secretly happy?"

He sort of smirked, squinted an eye at me.

Mom said, "Jail?"

"Hmm," Marie said. "And camp."

"Dad," I said, "here's a difference between you and me. You thought when we played the card game that I was trying to guess, or predict, the next card. But I was trying to change it. I wanted to influence what it would be. And I wasn't mindlessly cannonballing off the swing set, or *wishing* that I would land okay. I was suggesting to the ground that it accept me. I was willing that there was no difference between me and the ground."

He just looked at me, his eyes wide this time. I can guess now what he must have been thinking. That that was the dumbest thing he'd heard yet. He said, "Well, you're about as stubborn as the ground." Everybody laughed.

I hadn't intended to be laughed at again. Sitting there amongst our parents, I couldn't muster the feeling of being adult. Dad was acting as if nobody before him had discovered that people suffer in private, in public. He didn't know about all the days and nights I had agonized over Marie before she agreed to live the rest of her life with me, afraid she didn't really love me, afraid I wasn't good enough for her, afraid someone else would attract her, afraid I might never for some reason even see her or speak to her again. During the day I'm sure I maintained a placid demeanor, but at night I sobbed prayers into my pillow. If I could I would have whisked her away, but I didn't have the means. I worked as a waiter at a country club. Besides, we weren't the type of kids who would elope. She certainly wasn't. We respected our parents. We hoped to please them. We would depend on college loans and scholarships and part-time work. Love for her was my only strength. Sometimes it felt like a very weak strength. Hence the desperate prayers.

"Are you going to let me tell this story or not? Let me at least get to the point."

"I thought you had," Mom said, smiling.

Marie took my hand under the table and put it on her thigh, soft under the creamy nylon skirt she wore. "How did they save his arm, Mr. Fielding?" she asked.

"Oh, an orthopedic surgeon on duty ordered some X-rays. They got him prepped for surgery but found a way to manipulate the bones in his sleep without having to cut. He got to stay in the hospital overnight. The possibility of his getting the anesthesia was why he couldn't have any water, but a nurse did come by with a crinkled cup of chipped ice. By the time Beverly got home he was in a cast and happy. Seemed like a miracle after all my worry.

"Show your arms," Dad told me.

I slipped my hand from Marie's and placed my arms on the table. My forearms were long and lean and almost equally straight, soft black hairs shading the muscle.

Dad said, "How'd you get here, into the body of this handsome young man? When I dream about you, you are still four or five years old. And how can you be so in love? How can you know you want to get married? I myself never knew. Who are you?"

Mom got up and walked around the table, then play-slapped Dad on the back of the head. "You knew," she said.

"Well, maybe after you told me," he said, ducking in case she took another whack at him.

But she went into the kitchen. From there, she said, "And your point is?"

"It's not obvious?" Dad asked.

"It's not *too* obvious," Mr. Hargrove said. "You mean that life's serious business, right?"

Dad shrugged with one shoulder, leaned his head to that side. "Yeah. I guess."

Really, I couldn't believe all this moroseness about my broken arm, which was nothing compared to what Marie and her parents had gone through. During dinner, her mother had already recounted the story of Marie's survival of ovarian cancer. Marie had had a hysterectomy. She was out of school for two years. That's why she was older than me but in my graduating class. Her illness was what firmed her desire to be a doctor. Talk about serious business.

We already knew the broad facts. But Mom and Dad were, I think, just tonight realizing that they might never be grandparents if I married Marie, and they weren't anxious for me to get married in the first place. But I wasn't thinking about wanting children; Marie still had check-ups to confirm that she was in remission.

First, her mother had also told us about a dream she'd had before she knew she was pregnant with Marie. She saw herself raking leaves in their yard, where a smiling woman in a pale green dress approached and offered a wrapped present, the name "Marie" on the raspberry ribbon.

Dad must have been thinking about that now. He said, "Marie is the real miracle, huh? A real dream girl. You folks are a strong family."

That softened me toward Dad some. I suppose that by telling about my broken arm, he'd been trying to tell her parents that I was special, too. That he loved me as they loved her. Maybe he'd been trying to soften her parents toward me, show me as resilient, determined, so they would accept me—as I had wished of the ground during my flight from the swing.

Mom brought in a banana cream pie, cut into it, and served the ivory-colored plates.

Mr. Hargrove tasted a bite. He said, "Well, we certainly hadn't counted on an early marriage for Marie. And it has nothing to do with you, Ray. But if you can cook like your mother, that would be one less thing to worry about."

"Thank you, thank you," Mom said, chuckling. "He hangs around the kitchen sometime."

I wasn't sure what was happening. Were they giving us their blessings? If I could cook?

Dad said, "It's good to know what you want. And it's good to have a partner through life. Marriage *is* lifelong, you know. Supposed to be. I have some wishes and I have some hopes. I *know* you two don't know what you're doing, but I hope it works out."

"Hopes and wishes," Mrs. Hargrove sighed. She frowned at her pie.

Dad said, "Look, obviously we would prefer you two to wait. Marie, you're ambitious. Planning to go to medical school and all. Ray, by golly, you've already achieved a truly ambitious goal. Somehow, you've caused a girl as pretty and smart as Marie to want to marry you. But," he turned to her parents, "I know you don't want any more handicaps and obstacles for her."

He stopped then, leaving that statement hanging. He bowed his head toward his wedge of pie, as if he were about to say grace again before eating it. The light from our brass chandelier shone on his scalp. Surely we understood that I was the handicap and obstacle he meant. This angered me. While I waited for someone to speak in my defense, I held Marie's hand again. She dug into my palm a little, as if to urge me to speak up. The parents all looked lost in thought. I had the feeling all of a sudden that they weren't thinking about me. Or that maybe all this talk had them remembering their youth, when they were ambitious, and musing about whatever handicaps and obstacles they'd had to endure. Mom had managed to get her Master's degree when I was a baby, but never her Ph.D. Dad had to have wanted to do something besides be a modern-day butler in a rich white man's house. As far as I knew, Mrs. Hargrove had never worked outside of their home. And her husband, who did own a gas station, maybe he wished for a life that didn't have him wearing overalls every day. He'd been a football star in high school. But he'd dropped out of college when he discovered he needed to know how to read, which he learned to do, Marie told me, by taking classes at the Y after she was born. What misery and tears had they been hiding in public? Plus there were Marie and I, possibly drags on our parents' lives. We had to be. The money we cost them. The worry. It was the first time I'd considered myself that way. I sat there a minute and really wondered how I seemed to Dad, to all of them, but to Dad especially. Stubborn, shortsighted, foolish, young. Selfish? While I was on the other side of the table, having that out-of-body moment, I saw my thinness made narrower by both arms under the table now, my hands grasping Marie's. I saw a bright-eyed young dude with the slender frame of his mother, a boy with his mother's light-brown complexion. He had his mother's "forest creature eyes," as Dad said when he teased her. Tea-colored, narrow. I saw something in those eyes. Confusion and fear. Determination, desperation, and guilt. I was desperate to establish my life. I was determined to have Marie.

So even then I could see myself in third person, as I was instructed to do years later on the first day of writing class. For my sixteenth birthday, Dad had bought me the Pinto I wrote the sentence about. But no, I never wrecked it. It was slow and boring and embarrassingly new, though used. Within a year, the engine just seized up one day, leaving me frustrated and angry. Cheap piece of crap, smoke pouring from under the hood.

Marie said, "Mr. Fielding, I don't consider Ray a handicap to me. I consider him as much my future as every next day's sunrise."

He reared back in his chair. He had a barrel chest and a high round stomach, which he rubbed through the fabric of his tan knit shirt. He had a big, shiny bald head. When I was little I used to imagine he was a genie. "That's not exactly what I meant," he said. "You kids are launching yourselves too soon, throwing yourselves out there with no sure place to land—like Ray from that damn swing set. You don't know how frightening that is for us."

Marie said, "We do know how scary it is, Mr. Fielding. We are aware that you can never really know what will happen. Who would have predicted that Ray and I would fall in love? But we'll work jobs. We'll go to college. We'll still have you. We'll be helping each other, not handicapping."

"Why don't you just wait?"

"But why?" she asked.

The parents looked at each other. Mr. Hargrove struck a match and then blew it out. "Sorry," he said. They looked helpless and lost. Marie had that glow about her that I found so mysterious and irresistible.

Dad smiled and ruffled his mustache. Then he grinned. "Cannonball!" he called her in a booming voice that startled me. "You really knock me out!"

"Good heavens, Mel," Mom said.

I like ending this here, with Dad's long-winded echo of my old cannonball adventure. That was when he cleared the way—for me to be whoever I could think of to be.

Honeymoon

RAY AND MARIE HAD TALKED ABOUT THE MURDERS DURING THE weeks preceding the visit, and they hoped the murderer, or murderers, would be caught by the time they got here. The killings had been so astonishing, growing in number month to month, that Ray had tired of commenting about them. Always there were new reports of a missing kid and a discovered body. Or maybe Marie would bring it up late at night after he got home from work, or early in the morning as she left for her job, after she woke him up to do his assignments for school before leaving him grim in their apartment's silence—until he could wash his face, turn on some music, put some other sensations over his nausea about the mysterious deaths, over the gloom of starting the day morbidly, over the dread of needing to be responsible, to finish his homework.

By the time he had driven six hours from North Carolina, navigated the lanes of speeding, merging traffic on Atlanta's downtown connector, took the ramp for I-20 west, and exited onto Lakewood Freeway, he felt tense but relieved to finally be at his vacation destination with Marie. It was 1981. They had been married six months. They were taking Memorial Day weekend to have a quasi-honeymoon with Marie's beloved cousin Teen and Teen's husband Otis. Ray had met them only once, the wedding weekend in Durham.

Teen was the maid of honor. Otis had pitched in to be principal photographer when the one they hired suddenly got shingles.

They were older than Ray and Marie, in their late twenties, though closer to Marie's age, twenty-two, than to Ray, who was nineteen. Otis laughed a lot, even about getting ticketed for speeding during their drive to North Carolina for the ceremony. And Teen had a motherly quality, a consoling assurance that everything would be all right, fascinating to Ray from a woman so young.

One reason Ray and Marie were visiting now was that Teen was pregnant for the first time. This might be the only chance for Marie to see her in that fulsome condition. When they parked in front of the house, a moss-green bungalow with purple shutters and a neat yard, Teen came out the glass front door smiling with her arms spread wide. She wore a white, sleeveless maternity top and lavender shorts. Marie unclipped her seat belt and ran into her cousin's arms. They did a little dance on the concrete walkway bordered by red and purple impatiens, and Ray watched, confused by this sudden eruption of happiness that, after such an exhausting effort to get there, didn't seem to involve or include him. It took a moment before he remembered to get out of the car, too.

Teen hugged Ray and Ray petted her belly. Then, as Marie was pulling their suitcase from the hatchback, Otis drove up in their midnight-blue Riviera. He wore a red bandana knotted around his neck, under the collar of a denim, snap-button shirt. "What it is, Ray?" He grinned at Marie. "What's happening, good-looking? You thought you were guests, but you're home again."

In the kitchen, Ray and Marie sat on stools at a polished concrete-topped island. Teen took a cellophane-wrapped bowl from the refrigerator. "I hope you can eat shrimp, Ray," she said.

"I can eat it," he said. "You made it, I can definitely eat it."

"This is just an appetizer. A shrimp salad. We're having steaks as soon as Otis gets the grill going."

Otis took off his neckerchief and used it to wipe the tops of two cans of Budweiser he pulled from the refrigerator. He gave one to Ray.

Marie said, "Otis, take Ray somewhere tonight."

"We can all go out," he said. He faced them from the other side of the island, rested his arms on the top.

"Naw. Teen and I want to baby prep."

"Oh yeah? I thought I already did that." He winked at Ray.

Marie laughed. She hugged Ray's arm and leaned her head on his shoulder. Her long hair, combed in the car, tickled his chin. "You're bad," she said to Otis. "We're going to plan the nursery. In two months you're going to need a crib, a changing table, a diaper pail. What else, Teen?"

"A babysitter."

"Yeah, I wish that could be me," Marie said. "But for now I'm gonna help you decide how to decorate."

"Don't worry too much about that," Otis said. "Everything will be purple. Some kind of purple."

"So what?" Teen said, putting plates and forks on the countertop. "I like purple. When I can go back to work, I'm going to open a store that sells only purple things. I'm going to send out a call: where are all the purple people at? They will all come running to my store."

From the kitchen door, which was open, Ray saw they even had a purple backyard. Violets dotted the lawn, which was shallow but lush, the neighbors' houses shielded by a high wooden fence fronted by glossy green hedges, new leaves as bright and shiny as fresh paint. A deep purple hydrangea bloomed in a corner. Wisteria dangled over the back fence with fading lavender blossoms.

Just as Ray was thinking how funereal the color was, Teen said, "If you guys go out tonight, be careful. You know they found another body the other day."

Marie said, "We read about that one. He was older, right? Not a boy. Twenty-three. They think it's the same killer?"

"He's added to the list," Teen said. "The last few have been older. One theory is that the killer's appetite, or taste, has matured."

"Do you think we can talk about something else for a minute?" Otis said. He put down his beer can and frowned.

"Otis, they're grabbing people your age. That last guy was near your age. Sometimes you stay out until four in the morning. I don't know when it's going to be you who never comes home."

"I always come home, darling. I'm home now. I'll stay home tonight if you want."

"What are you doing out until four in the morning, Otis?" Marie asked.

"I have a buddy who runs a club off Old National. I help out sometimes. Extra moola, you know. It's where I would take us tonight, or Ray since ya'll want to hang tight. Nobody is getting abducted from any nightclubs, Teen."

"Not yet. As far as we know."

"We don't have to go out," Ray said.

"It's cool, Ray. Really."

The guest bedroom was cozy—a high, iron bed painted silver, covered with a textured lavender spread and piled at the head with pillows of violet and silk. At the window, lavender blinds showed slices of yard and the sunny street. Ray could see his brown Corolla parked at the curb. He pushed their suitcase onto the rug and pulled Marie to the bed with him. He stroked her arm. Her brown skin looked warm and beautiful in the lavender light, against the lavender spread.

"Marie," he said. "You look valuable. I believe Teen really, really likes purple."

She snickered. "She's a purple extremist. Remember, she tried to get me to use purple for our wedding color? Lord, *she* had a purple wedding."

"You make purple look all right." He snuggled closer to her, kissed her neck.

"We need to save this for later, Ray."

"You smell too good."

"Like lilacs?"

"Maybe, yeah. Grapes. I don't want to go anywhere tonight without you," he said.

"You go and have a good time. You deserve it, Ray. Besides, I really want the girl time with Teen."

He lay on his back and stared at the ceiling fan. It had iridescent bulbs. He was thinking of the night before their wedding. He and Otis had been a two-man bachelor party. Otis came to town and somehow found a hot bright club full of naked women, when all Ray had planned was to shine his shoes and try to sleep before the next night's ceremony. Ray watched the entertainment Otis paid for—a short brown stripper who sat at their table or brought them drinks when it wasn't her turn to be on the stage. Every so often she would get up and bend over in front of them where they sat, showing her wiggling bare butt, and Otis slipped dollar bills under the pink lace garter that strapped her thigh. Ray had never seen a woman's nudity from that angle, up close. When he put money in her garter, it was like feeding strange food to a strange and needy animal. He felt confused to be so publicly aroused. And guilty, too. They stayed at the club until it closed. And now, instead of being worried that someone would abduct and kill him, Ray worried Otis would want to show off some Atlanta strip joint.

"What about the honeymoon?" he asked Marie, embarrassed, because if this was a honeymoon, it was a pitiful one.

"When you come back, sweetie."

Weeks before today, Ray figured out that the parade of deaths had been advancing since his marriage—that while he and Otis had been laughing with naked women on the wedding eve, and while he and Marie were shaking through their vows the next day, and for each month since, some child lay dead and undiscovered in Atlanta. But he hadn't told Marie about his calculation. It disturbed him that he had made the connections, and he didn't want the historical marker of their marriage to be serial death. He thought he could ignore the correlation, and he didn't want her to have to. Not that she couldn't figure it for herself.

Besides, theirs wasn't the only marriage begun during this time. And there were other atrocities occurring simultaneously around the world. It couldn't mean that all these new marriages were doomed. But he sometimes wondered if he would ever remember their beginning without the memory of this revulsion. Just yesterday, he had stared at the pictures of the dark faces of the dead boys in a news magazine and had felt a dreary nausea. His head ached. It was as if pain and evil were in the ink that told the story and formed the images of the children. He threw the magazine out.

That night, leaving Marie and Teen to baby furniture catalogues and books of meaningful first and middle names, Otis took Ray to a few clubs on the way to the one Otis helped to manage. Each was a dance club, no strippers; at least no strippers stripping. The women were dressed up, made up, looking like models. The men looked like models too, in suits, some flashier than others, with Jheri curls, diamond jewelry. Otis wore a medium blue suit with a pale pink spread-collar shirt. Ray made do with a cheap sports coat he'd bought to vary his attire for church—a stiff gray jacket that curled up at the back hem as if it was made of construction paper. It was of a fuzzy weight too warm for this May weather, less than a hundred dollars, tapered cut. Now he wondered why anybody would even make such a poor-quality coat, and why anybody would sell it. Riding in Otis's Riviera, he looked down at the purple handkerchief Teen had fluffed in his breast pocket before they left the house. "You look handsome," she'd said.

They were on a wide boulevard with all the traffic signals synchronized and turning green as Otis sped under them. "I've got a surprise for you," he said. "We're gonna run by my girl's crib for a minute. Might be somebody there for you to meet."

"What?"

"A friend of my girl's. Her name is Ruth. I've been calling but the line's busy. I know she's expecting us, though."

"You have a girl named Ruth?" He was trying to understand how Otis had a daughter that had never before been mentioned, and how she could be expecting them at this hour. It was already after midnight. She'd be what, a baby? Like, six at the most?

"My girl's name is Cleo. Your girl's name is Ruth," Otis said.

"Aw, Otis," Ray said, understanding now. "My girl's name is Marie. What about Teen? What about them?"

Otis steered onto the interstate expressway. He lit a cigarette. He still had his drink from the last club, a plastic brandy snifter tucked between his legs. "I don't know, Ray. I know you're in love and everything. I mean, I am too. You don't have to do anything if you don't want to. It's just that Ruth is a little freak and, you know, you might get lucky."

"A super freak?" Ray laughed.

"I got a sense for these things," Otis said. "I can just tell."

At the club they had just left, a woman had pranced all over the dance floor shouting, "Walk that dog, walk that damn dog" well after the song had ended, until a man in a lime blazer got her and sat her down. Still, she hollered, "Walk that motherfucking dog." She was some kind of freak, tall and skinny in a glittering blue dress with a glittering blue beret on her head.

But maybe this Ruth was a purple freak like Teen. Maybe she liked to smell feet. Maybe she had flippers instead of feet.

"Hey, Otis, I appreciate it, but that's not what I need right now."

"Hell, you need it. We're men, Ray. I mean Marie is a pretty girl and no doubt a good wife, but…"

Ray cut his eye at Otis. He could guess what Otis was thinking: that Marie was the first girl Ray had had sex with, and she could be the last if Ray persisted with this naïve devotion to monogamy.

"You know what, Ray, and I don't mean this as a criticism. I admire you, man. But you got married young, okay? I mean, I thought I got married young. I was twenty-one, deep in love, too—like you. Teen, she is my absolute friend, incredibly sexy, and fun. Not to mention soon the mother of my baby. But I can think of someone else besides Teen. I always could. You can still only think of Marie. You just need to be prepared for when you don't."

"And you think Ruth the freak can prepare me?"

"You never know. But hey man, I can respect your commitment. Don't be afraid, that's all, when and if you need to step out. We're going over there just the same."

"It's already late, man."

"I don't want Teen to start expecting me home by midnight. Besides, we're supposed to stay out late. I'm entertaining you, right?"

"Right."

For the first time since marrying Marie, Ray felt his youth was a liability. He had argued to his parents and hers, to anybody who questioned him, that both he and Marie were old enough, mature enough, responsible enough to be in love and to be married. During an adolescence of anxiety and uncertainty about just why he'd been born, it had come as a relief to know he was meant to be her partner. On the other hand, he had not, it seemed, lived long enough to experience anything Otis was talking about. He'd read about it, of course, relationships in literature, works that, as his English professor asserted, "probed the mysteries of extraordinary and desperate human hearts." In real life such a heart just seemed sleazy. That anybody he knew, or that he, could actually move toward someone other than his wife was surprising. And he was not prepared for it. He wondered about his father, and Marie's father, his English professor, and the minister who had presided over their wedding. Was this why they had said he was too young? Did they expect he should learn first that he might cheat on his wife?

"Otis, how do you know Ruth is a freak? What about your girl, Cleo?"

"Radar. Teen and Marie have a little freakiness, too. Also, their mamas. I can just tell. But I have this theory that every woman freaks for the right dude. Some are just more ready than others."

It was 12:40 when Otis wove through short streets behind some public housing and pulled up at a boxy house on a lot below street level. They parked at the curb and walked down the driveway to the front door.

A plump, freckled woman opened the door. She seemed breathless. Tears spilled from her light brown eyes when she grabbed Otis by the arm. "Oh, Otis, thank you, *thank* you for being here. I don't know where Jeff is. He's just not anywhere and I've been calling everybody." She tugged him into the house and Ray followed. "He's missing."

"What do you mean, he's missing?" Otis said.

"I'm about to go nuts. I've got the damn police on the phone now. Shit, shit, shit. I should have—I don't know what I should have done. I mean he was supposed to go home with his school friend. And his fucking asshole daddy is nowhere to be found."

She led them quickly down a hall to the kitchen, where she picked up a phone from the counter and started talking, apologizing to the person on the line, saying, "No, sir, that wasn't him at the door. It was a friend of mine."

Otis hugged her from behind, stopped her from wrapping herself in the stretched white cord from the wall. She wore a loose green dress and yellow flip-flops. She had long, coarse, reddish hair braided into pigtails that curled forward under her ears. Otis rested his chin on top of her head.

Ray listened while she explained to the policeman that Jeff, her son, was supposed to have gone home with a schoolmate but for some reason did not. When she got home from work about nine and the boy didn't call her as they had planned, she called the schoolmate's family but got no answer. She guessed they had all gone to a movie, or skating, and maybe to eat. But when she called last around ten, the family was home but Jeff wasn't with them. Jeff had told the boy at school that the plan had changed, that he wasn't spending the night with them after all. For the past two hours she'd been on the phone trying to find him, calling his teachers, schoolmates. She said she hoped now he was with his father, but she couldn't reach him either.

Ray looked at an opened address book on top of an opened city directory on the counter, a glass of dark wine by the yellow enamel sink, a chrome breadbox, shiny ceramic canisters in the shapes of a rooster, a hen, and a chick. The house was cold from air conditioning.

The doorbell rang, followed quickly by a knock. Cleo turned to Ray, seeming to notice him for the first time. Otis gestured with his head, and Ray said, "I'll get it."

At the door was a thin, dark woman holding a small paper bag. She didn't seem surprised to see Ray. "Did you find Jeff?" she asked.

"No. Not yet." He backed up to let her in.

"You must be Ray. I'm Ruth." She held out her hand and Ray shook it. Bangles jangled on her wrist. "I'm glad you guys got here. Cleo was about to lose it. I went home to get something to calm her." She showed him the bag, pulled out a prescription bottle.

"Oh," Ray said.

They stepped into the hall to see Cleo and Otis in their kitchen embrace, Cleo still on the phone. Ruth led Ray into another room, the living room, where she sat on a sofa and Ray took a chair opposite.

"So, you know what's going on?" she asked. "Cleo's been calling all around and fearing the worst." She hugged herself and seemed to shudder.

A five-by-seven framed photo of a boy was on the table next to Ruth, as was a glass Ruth quickly picked up. The glass held melting ice and a stranded slice of lime.

"I'm sure Jeff's okay," she said, "probably with his dad—if we could locate him. But right now Jeff's just gone."

Ray nodded. "Is that him?"

She looked toward the door. "Where? Oh, this." She touched the photo. "Yes. He's a good boy, you know? A good kid. I mean willful, but good. So maybe he just ran away or something. But he ought to know what this is doing to his mama."

He was a regular-looking kid, wearing a red rugby shirt with a white collar, smiling. His image looked much more clear and vivid than those black-and-white pictures of murdered boys in the newspaper and magazines. Those pictures had a blurred quality, as if taken entirely for the purpose of expressing death. But Jeff looked alive.

Ruth said, "Every kid they've killed was somebody's son, and the son of somebody's friend. I mean, there is reason to be hysterical if we choose to be, or if we can't help it."

Ray didn't say anything. He gazed at Ruth, who looked down into her watery glass. She had on a satin black tank top and black pants and black patent leather loafers. Her silver bangles glinted. She wore eye makeup and lipstick, and perfume. Not a lot, but Ray noticed. Had she made herself shiny and fragrant for him?

He could hear Cleo's voice as she spoke on the phone, but not exactly what she was saying. Finally, he said, "I didn't know Cleo had a son," as if he had even known Cleo.

"Yeah. He's just eleven." She walked to the door, looked down the hall, then sat again. "I got here a while ago and found her like this. I mean she's trying to control the panic, as you would imagine. Kids are just stupid." She laughed.

"She's talking to the police now."

"I think that's the right thing. I mean it's the best thing."

After a moment, Ray got up to look down the hall. Cleo was off the phone and crying softly on Otis's chest. He held her, seemed to be whispering to her.

"You want a drink?" Ruth said. She moved to open a door on the wall-length entertainment cabinet. A television and stereo system sat above a shelf of liquor bottles and glasses and a red ice bucket.

Ray took a moment to assess his sobriety. He'd drunk a couple of beers out with Otis. He felt okay, though—fear for the missing kid, and the earlier fear of Ruth, seemed to have dissolved the buzz he'd been feeling. He wondered if the police were on the way, and if Otis intended to be here when they came. He wanted to go home. He wanted the boy found and he wanted to get back to Otis's house.

Ruth dropped ice in the glasses. Her dark shoulders were smooth and toned. She had a short Afro. He tried to see the freak in her, but he didn't know what to look for. Her walk was ordinary, little movement in her hips that flared out from her small, belted waist. Her eyes shone. Maybe it was the bangles. He couldn't know—didn't have the radar, he decided. He wondered instead, where is that boy? He wondered if Marie was asleep or awake.

Ruth gave him his drink and sat again across from him. They were silent for a while. She said, "Is your drink okay?"

He said that it was, although he hadn't tasted it.

She asked, "So you are Otis's cousin? From Carolina?"

"Yes. Actually, my wife and his wife are cousins." Then he wondered if he should have mentioned their being married. But surely she knew about Otis.

"It's a shame this horror that's happened to this city. Everything is tainted with gloom and suspicion. When Cleo invited me over I was pretty excited to get to meet someone new, from out of town. Maybe break this spell. My husband—well, I'm married, too. But he doesn't love me. You know, I mean, we're not very happy. I mean to say that it's okay if you're married—I knew that. Believe me, I understand now that it means nothing, necessarily." She got up and went to the stereo. "God, I hope Jeff is all right."

"It must mean something," Ray said.

"I said necessarily. Almost everybody I know is messing around. Maybe you love your wife. And she loves you. Yet you're here, meeting me."

"I hadn't planned on it."

"It's an accident, huh?"

"Otis set it up. I didn't ask him to."

"Fair enough. I'm glad, though. But you look too young to be married."

He recognized the music: Miles Davis's *Kind of Blue*. The tune was "So What?" He almost said that title aloud in response to Ruth's comment about his age. It's what Teen had said about her liking the color purple.

Ray swirled his drink, pushed the lime slice down into the liquid with his finger. He felt a sudden disassociation. He thought about guys he used to be friends with but, since he'd been married, never saw anymore. It seemed just as easy now to break from any relationship. He wasn't related to Otis. He wasn't related to Teen. Marie, in Ruth's eyes, was probably a strange girl attached to him, a girl he found himself having to defend being with.

He said, "It's not like I'm a hobo traveling with crocodile luggage."

"What on earth does that mean?" Ruth asked.

He laughed, shook his head. He sipped his vodka. Even his parents, who had sobbed at his wedding, seemed separated from him, arrayed against him as they were when he said he wanted to get married, and seeming still to reproach him. And he felt no compelling attraction to Ruth. He had a thought about the missing boy—either kidnapped or run away, feeling too the easy disconnection, that no relationship was real, defined him, or determined his fate. Was the kid feeling elated and free or terrified, Ray wondered. It seemed almost like clairvoyance.

Ray got up again to peek down the hall. Otis and Cleo were no longer in the kitchen. They came out of another door in the hallway, found Ray standing there. Otis introduced her to Ray, and Ray said he believed everything was going to turn out fine. "Are the police looking?" he asked.

Cleo shrugged, sobbed. "They're supposed to come by here and get a picture." She was short. Her face was shiny. She held a wad of tissue with both hands against her chest.

"We'll look for him," Otis said. He kissed her forehead. He then leaned into the living room to wave to Ruth, who leapt up and walked with them to the front door. Ray couldn't say, "It was nice to meet you," and Ruth couldn't say, "Enjoy the rest of your visit." They didn't say anything. Ray drained his drink, and he and Otis got back into the car.

Otis revealed they were headed to Cleo's ex-husband's house. "The prick's not answering his phone," he said.

"Where is that?"

"Not too far. Besides, we needed to get out of Cleo's before the cops came. Next thing you know, we're suspects if anything really bad has happened. Cops calling at my house, getting Teen upset. Can't have that."

The dashboard clock read 1:12. They drove a long way out on I-20, into Rockdale County, and got off in Conyers at the Salem Road exit. After a few more turns Ray couldn't say where they were. They slowed in front of a dark brick house with a ragged, weedy yard. Broken cement pocked the empty driveway. The garage door was closed. No lights anywhere. Even the streetlight in front of the house went out as they parked.

"I'm thinking he should be home," Otis said. "If he was gone, he'd probably have left a light on somewhere. Wouldn't you?"

Ray and Marie had left two lights on at their apartment. They had delayed leaving that morning because they couldn't decide which lights. "Yeah," he said. "A small light inside somewhere."

"Right. Something a thief might see if one was looking."

"A porch light, maybe."

"At least."

"The doorbell button is lit, though." It was an amber dot in the darkness.

Otis turned toward him and laughed. "Good eye."

"Thanks."

Otis turned back to study the ex-husband's house. Ray looked over at a house across the street. As he watched, a light in the back-yard came on. "The light over there just came on," he said.

Otis grunted.

"Do you know Jeff's father?"

"Poke? Yeah. But he doesn't know about me. I mean he knows me, but—you know what I mean." He took the keys from the ignition and dropped them in his jacket pocket. "Cleo married him when she was still in high school, pregnant. He was older than us, in the Army."

He opened his door and the overhead light illuminated the car's tan interior. "I'm gonna check it out." He shut the door quietly, pushing it with his hip, and moved down the slight slope of driveway to the garage, where he peered through that window awhile, then made his way to the front door and peeked in the small window there. Ray did a quick calculation: if Jeff was eleven, then Cleo must have been no more than fifteen when he was born, when she got married. And the daddy, Poke, was probably a Vietnam vet.

Ray adjusted the rearview mirror to see behind the car. Someone was walking toward them, a distant figure moving in the shadow between streetlights. Ray turned back to look for Otis but didn't see him anywhere; he had moved away from the front door.

The figure behind him moved into the bluish light pouring from the nearest lit lamp. It was a black man in a white lab coat, a small white dog on a leash in front of him. Walk that dog, Ray thought, remembering the woman at the club. The man came out of the light into the darkness that extended to and enveloped the car. Ray ducked down in his seat. Why was anyone walking a dog at this hour? Why was he wearing a lab coat? Then he thought, where is Otis?

Ray had read a disturbing theory that the Center for Disease Control was responsible for the murders, using blood elements from the young males to research a cancer-fighting drug. Something about sickle cell and interferon. It was a wild theory published in the letters section of his college newspaper. But boys were being killed for some reason. And Ray entertained the fantasy that maybe the man walking his dog had abducted Jeff. The man was a mad scientist, taking a break from killing boys and extracting from them valuable genes and tissue. Maybe his associates had grabbed Otis. Or maybe Otis had broken into the house.

When Ray raised up, the backyard light of the house across the street was out again. A motion light, he decided. A cat or squirrel triggering it? It went on again. Otis was not visible at the ex-husband's house. The dim white lab coat disappeared down the street. Ray got out of the car. He stood against it, peering at Poke's house. The white paint in the dark morning mist looked ghostly. Then he stepped into the driveway.

A netless basketball goal listed in grass to the left of the garage. He peeked into the garage window as Otis had done. A car—a dark Honda—was parked there. He looked through the window of the front door and saw nothing at first, and then barely made out a long mirror hung over a pale fireplace. The mirror reflected bits of light from the backyard across the street and allowed Ray to see dark furniture in the room. What if Otis *had* broken in? But Ray could detect no sign of—activity, the word he settled on, to avoid "no sign of life."

He turned to the street. They weren't going to find Jeff out here tonight, he realized. If he were really a victim, dead, they wouldn't find him. Ray wouldn't even be able to tell Marie that he knew the boy's mother, that he'd searched for him. He'd be required to protect Otis. He wondered about Otis, a guy who could have a mistress without guilt, with a sense of entitlement, who could maybe know personally the victim of a serial killer.

It seemed that Ray knew only teachers and churchgoers in Durham. He didn't know his college classmates at all. His coworkers at the country club were mostly older, career waiters who talked about their own children in college. And the people they served were doctors, lawyers, businessmen, architects—some who drank too much but whose money and privilege made them simultaneously mysterious and boring. Maybe they, too, had affairs, but everybody he knew at home seemed predictable and tame, doing exactly what was expected of them.

He couldn't believe he was here, standing at a strange door in the cooling wee hours, looking out at a dark, monochromatic street, caught in this absurd search. Caught in history, he realized. That the boy could actually be the victim of a killer took his breath. His chest felt squeezed. Everything about this seemed unreal. He couldn't understand why he wasn't in bed with Marie. He should be feeling warmth from her sleeping body in its blue cotton gown, on those lavender sheets. Her skin was an unsurpassed comfort for him, as if it alone were the source of her life, her love, her heat. He felt cheated now, manipulated and guilty—guilty because this absence from her was important, if useless.

He hoped Otis hadn't broken into the house. That would make Ray an accessory somehow. He could be arrested, implicated in the boy's disappearance—or murder—though he was innocent. To erase that thought, he focused on breathing. He breathed deeply and imagined Jeff doing the same thing. Where was he? Soaked in piss on some car's backseat? In the trunk? Wet and cold and curled against a muddy riverbank?

Otis made a scraping noise at the corner of the house that made Ray jump. "Damn, Otis," he gasped. "Where'd you go?"

"You all right?"

"Where were you? I thought you had gotten inside."

"Out back." He walked over to where Ray stood at the front door. "Dude's got two sheds out there."

"Yeah?"

"Nothing. Junk."

"We're not really helping, Otis. We should be home, and the police should be looking for Jeff."

Otis didn't respond. He rubbed his eyes. He said, "This worries me. The best case is that Poke kidnapped him, but Poke could be at some club, or anywhere. If Jeff's not here, I don't know where he is."

"Did you ring the doorbell?"

"Of course I rang the doorbell."

A car turned onto the street a block away. It stopped at the corner, its headlights seeming to stare. Then it made its way slowly up the street, accelerating a little, slowing again. It finally pulled to a stop beside Otis's car, backed up and moved forward beside it again. Suddenly, something came flying over the roof of the Riviera and landed on the yard.

"Jesus. It's just the fucking paper man," Otis said.

"The dewy news," Ray said.

"The daily news," Otis corrected.

"Yeah. I was joking."

"Okay."

"You think we ought to get out of here?"

They watched the car's taillights diminish to red points before they stepped away from the stoop. Ray stared at the newspaper, sheathed in plastic, a fat pale lump in the dark weeds.

Back in the car, Otis drove slowly around the neighborhood. After a couple of turns, they saw the man in the white lab coat walking his little white dog. The man wore glasses, and he looked at them as they drove by. "Insomniac," Otis said.

He kept driving, roaming the blocks, as if they would find Jeff walking along at this hour. Ray looked out on the dark houses, the dim lawns, the dull cars in the driveways and parked along the curbs. He tried to picture Marie in Cleo's place, alone and distraught with a missing child and absent, horrible husband. But he could only see Cleo like that. He closed his eyes.

When he opened them again, they were speeding on I-20. Actually, they were quickly decelerating as Otis exited at Cascade. It was 2:59. Ray wasn't sure he had slept. He remembered the sound of wind, thought he'd been conscious of it all the way. Before long they were cruising up to Cleo's house where all the house lights were on and two police cars claimed the curbs. Otis kept driving past. "I should call," he said.

He drove to a nearby gas station and used the payphone near the street. Ray watched him for a while in the light of the bulb in the telephone booth, the red traffic signal bleeding onto the booth's blue glow, Otis bathed in an imperfect purple. It meant either royalty or death. King Otis and dead Jeff? Yeah, maybe this town was full of freaks. Ray's insight went no further, stopped at the blunt wall of being up all night. Marie, Ray thought, would be swathed in those significant sheets now, maybe dreaming of being a doctor, closing wounds, resuscitating hearts. That was her ambition. How necessary she was. Otis had one hand in his pants pocket, his coattail pushed back so that, head bent over the receiver, he looked like a man in an ad, purposeful and poised, candid and posed—*What Sort of Man Reads Playboy?* It occurred to Ray, *I'm the freak in this town.*

Ray closed his eyes again. He felt an extraordinary struggle in his heart; he felt a hard hope that the boy had been found, amid a reluctant hatred for Otis. He had a vision of the phone booth swarming with wasps, Otis maddeningly untouched and unconcerned. Yet Ray didn't want Otis to be punished. Not really. He wanted to get out of the car, back to Marie, or back to somewhere familiar.

Gifted

MARIE SAW SOMETHING IN ME, I GUESS, BUT IT WASN'T WHAT I thought she was paying attention to. I thought she liked my ardent love for her. That was nearly all I knew of myself. But what she saw must have been something I failed to develop sufficiently, some promise of what she could love about me. A mystery.

We were too young. Everybody said so. Except us. We should be together, she said. Why should we be apart? I said.

My father cried at the wedding. First time I'd seen that. So many people cried. Imagine a young couple, recently graduated from high school, beautifully dressed at the altar of the church, terrified and bewildered not just by their commitment to each other but by the tears of their parents and other relatives. Embarrassed, the bride and groom look at each other and laugh, showing the hopeless youth that has so moved and frightened the grown-ups. This, before the vows had even begun.

Tears during the recessional, but smiles at the reception. Lots of weak congratulations and resigned advice. I wasn't even old enough to legally drink the champagne. Marie and I had graduated in June and now it was September. It was two weeks after my eighteenth birthday. Marie had turned twenty in April. We were toasted and wished every happiness. My father pulled me aside and said, ominously, "A woman can be satisfied with love only so long." He looked me in the eye and nodded meaningfully, but I didn't know what he meant. He would be dead in two years, but not before Marie and I divorced.

My mother's brother, Uncle Algernon, explained domestic happiness to me. "With your Aunt Luanne and me, whoever sees that something needs to be done just does it. Taking out the trash, washing the dishes or laundry, cooking or cleaning. Doesn't matter. Washing the car, mowing the lawn. Whatever. We get along great, thirty years."

Uncle Del, my father's brother, found me as I came out of the bathroom. He walked with me back into the hotel ballroom and slipped me an envelope containing fifty dollars. He said, "Don't ever screw one of her friends. Next to money, that's the biggest cause of trouble." I looked across the rose-colored carpet at white-gowned Marie, surrounded by her bridesmaids in pale blue, and her mother in royal blue, and wondered what advice she was getting. Who could know? I doubted it was anything like I'd heard, most of which I felt I shouldn't share with her. That well-meaning counsel already was a secret separating us.

We had an apartment, an upstairs one-bedroom with a long hallway leading to a sunny, spacious kitchen, in a section of town between our parents' neighborhoods. Because we had no money, we got good financial aid to college, and I went to Central during the day and then worked nights at the country club. Marie had a job admitting patients at the hospital and took night classes at Carolina. We paid our rent, had a little left over for food, and depending on my tips we could decorate around our donated and flea-market furniture with plants and rugs, or picnic at Kerr Lake, go to a movie. Before we were married, we used to read to each other over the phone from books that we liked.

Mostly, Marie liked to visit. On Sundays after church, which I seldom attended on the excuse that I'd worked until two o'clock in the morning, we would go to her parents' house or to mine, or to the home of old-folk friends of hers, people I barely knew. They called me Gray or Roy instead of Ray, and called Marie Mary or Maggie. Close enough. We sat in their living rooms and drank Coke or tea, ate stale cake or chips. Often we'd stop first at the grocery store and buy a cluster of flowers for them, and at our next visit the flowers would be dry and dead still in the vase Marie had put them in. The visits had charm, but I never wanted to go. I wanted to rest at home with Marie. Watch a game with her.

That was a problem. Little I wanted reflected well on me. But who could fault Marie for wanting to cheer up old people?

We spent so little time together that whatever we had in common we couldn't nourish, while she at least was having her passion for science and medicine steadily fed, subjects I cared about only because Marie did.

We had mornings. Young husband in sunny kitchen slicing pink grapefruit and brewing coffee in one of two Mr. Coffees given at the wedding. Oatmeal, toast, and bacon. Young wife, sleepy and beautiful in the morning light, wants an egg. She puts ketchup on the egg.

"Marie," he asks, exaggerating revulsion, "how did you learn that ketchup might enhance an egg?"

"Bad for me, but good, too. Mmm." She smiles. "A sugar jolt."

"A gory plate."

Of his oatmeal with butter she says, "You're defeating the purpose of oatmeal, Ray. High cholesterol is the leading cause of heart disease and stroke, especially among black males. You need to live a long time."

"What about your eggs?" he says.

"Only three yolks a week. The safe limit."

"But oatmeal's awful without something. There's nothing we can eat."

"Sure there is." She's pre-med, taking a nutrition class. "The soy thing. Tofu."

He makes a face. He misses his mother's fried chicken.

Marie's shoulders shine in the sun through windows framed by white curtains, curtains with eyelet flowers embroidered in pink, yellow, green. Her suppleness when he encircles her waist and pulls her close. Maybe he could eat tofu.

We seldom had an evening meal together. It was cheaper for me to eat at the country club for free, save on the grocery bill. Marie often went to her mother's or ate spaghetti alone at our kitchen dinette while she studied before heading off to UNC. I studied in the library between classes, fraternized with busboys and other waiters at the country club, tried to do homework there. I was that guy then, deflecting both praise and criticism when found reading a book, absorbing the interest of people I served who wanted to know about me, and placidly accepting my invisibility to the others.

Marie and I both missed the ballgames, concerts, step shows, and extracurricular lectures. But after Marie's classes there were sometimes those who didn't want to go home, and Marie eventually accepted invitations to grab coffee. Her teacher often led those groups. Her academic advisor. What he saw: smart and gorgeous, and gorgeous and smart. The teacher hated going home; he was going through a divorce.

Marie won an "outstanding freshman" award given by the biology department. This was three weeks before her birthday. To celebrate all of it, I invited our families, her professor, a few of her friends, some old folks, and my coworker Romeo. He said his mother named him. He would tell me about his recent yearlong adventures in Mexico, Morocco, and London, where he claimed to have waited tables, played in bands, and survived as a gigolo. I thought he'd be funny to

Marie, as he was to me. He had dark, chin-length hair that fell across his face in a wave, and he traded on his racial and sexual ambiguity, flirting with both female and male patrons at the restaurant, and all the staff, black and white, Asian and Indian. Many people came nightly just to be served by him. He was black, and straight, I think, but for everybody he flashed his white teeth and swept back his wave of hair. I liked him. He didn't brag about his tips.

I invited Marie's professor so I could get a look at him, and because he had nominated her for the award. It shouldn't have shocked me to see he was white, but it did. I don't think she knew yet that I was jealous of him. Anyway, she talked about him constantly. She found it sad that his wife had moved to Wisconsin with their children. She admired his focus, his talent for teaching, and his encouraging counsel.

It wasn't a surprise party. But I wouldn't let Marie do anything to help. My mother was doing the cooking, and Marie's mother was baking a cake. But when I came home the night before, ready to tidy the apartment, I found Marie had already swept the floors and vacuumed the rugs. There were fresh hand towels in the bathroom, potpourri in a small bowl on the toilet tank, and votive candles on the sink, the living-room tables, and the dresser in the bedroom. On the bed, Marie had open schoolbooks and dresses from the closet. She had been cleaning and studying, and was now deciding what she would wear.

"I thought I was going to do the cleaning," I said.

"You can still clean the oven," she said. "And mop the kitchen."

It was past midnight. I had planned to bring the kitchen to an all-around shine when Marie went to church in the morning. Everybody would be heading here after church. I hadn't thought about the oven. Marie held up a peach-colored sundress. It still had the store tags on it, and I remembered when we had bought it on sale during the fall. Marie looked good in all the clothes she wore, but I was especially fond of dresses and blouses that bared her shoulders.

"I like that one. You finally get to wear it," I said. I pushed some books aside and lay down on the bed. It was a four-poster bed we bought at a flea market and lacked a canopy.

Tonight at work, one of the older waiters had talked to me about working for him in the business he was starting. He was putting together a team of waiters to contract out to hotels in the Triangle for banquet service. I mentioned this to Marie, that it could mean more money, especially if I started gradually, worked with him when I could, and then maybe, if he looked secure enough, quit the country club.

Marie didn't say anything at first. She was standing in the closet, her back to me, and I wondered if she had heard me. Then she said, "Waiting tables is waiting tables."

"I know." I studied her back. She had on cutoff sweatpants and a T-shirt. "But this guy is black."

"So?" She turned to face me. She looked annoyed. Maybe she was tired. Maybe she felt stressed. She wasn't showing any excitement about the party.

"So it might be more comfortable working for a black man for a change. And it wouldn't hurt to help a brother get a business going."

"Why does the brother have to have a waiter business?"

"I don't know, Marie. I mean, he's worked at the club for maybe twenty years. I guess it's the work he knows."

"That's the problem, Ray." She gathered up a group of dresses from the bed and hugged them to her chest. "He's carrying on the tradition of black people as America's servant class. It's as though the only businesses we can start are the butler business and the shoeshine business. Besides Mutual and the bank, everything else is a barbecue joint or a T-shirt kiosk. You're talking about a guy who's figured how to get paid to be the boss house-slave."

"Jesus, Marie." I'd never heard her speak so critically. She hung a few dresses in the closet.

"You can do better, Ray," she said.

"I'm trying to do better. That's what I'm talking about. I don't have time to do better than…better."

She stared at me awhile, as if thinking that over. Then she turned to hang up more clothes.

"I guess you don't want me to take the job," I said.

She sighed. "I guess I don't care, Ray. As I said, waiting tables is waiting tables."

"Well, damn," I said. "It's not like I'm the one starting the business. I'm just trying to afford to live."

I got off the bed and went into the kitchen to look at the oven. My mother would be using it to warm the party food. I took out the racks and sprayed the inside with cleaner. Then I mopped the kitchen floor, waited for it to dry, and waxed it. By the time I was finished, Marie was asleep. I hoped she would feel better in the morning. I hoped I would. I showered and slipped into bed. I inhaled the chemical stench of floor wax until I went to sleep.

In the afternoon, Marie came home from church with her parents. My parents came next, with trays and pots of food. Two of the old couples arrived together, and Romeo showed up at the same time as two of Marie's girlfriends. Marie's professor arrived late and Marie and her mother promptly moved to make him feel welcome. He wore a red polo shirt and pleated khakis. His hair was brown with blond streaks. He was in his thirties, shorter than me, but with a broad chest and stance. He carried a wrapped gift for Marie, yet the women fussed over him as if he were the honored one. The small apartment was packed, people in our living room, camped in the bedroom, and hanging out in the kitchen. My mother gave him a plate of turkey, corn, and collard greens. "Here you are, Professor, have a seat at the table." She gave him the place where she'd been sitting. The table sat only four.

"Thank you. This all looks great. Please, call me Jack," he said.

Marie, her mother, and my mother gathered around him, while my father and father-in-law went down the back stairs to smoke. I don't think Romeo was used to competition for female attention. He seemed no match for the professor. I got us a couple of beers and we stood and watched the talk for a while. The mothers took turns eliciting praise for Marie, and finally got to asking Jack about himself. "I grew up near Chicago," he said, his voice nasal and tenor. "I did my doctoral work at Princeton, and I've taught at North Carolina four years."

"Are you tenured?" my mother asked. A teacher herself, at the community college, she knew the important credential.

"Not yet." He smiled. "I apply next year. I've co-authored a book and it will be published by then. And hopefully, students like Marie will keep making me look good."

"We're really proud of her," Marie's mother said. "And we're tremendously grateful for what you've done for her."

He chuckled. "About all I've done is be amazed. I hope my daughters will grow up as talented as Marie. They live with their mother and I miss them. They're six and three. You're so lucky to have had Marie her whole life."

"We're lucky Marie is even alive," her mother said. "You know about her cancer recovery?"

"Mom," Marie said. "I told him. But let's not talk about that."

"I just want him to know you're not just smart; you're strong, too. A survivor. I hope your daughters are as special as Marie, too, Professor."

"Ray, would you get Professor Rigsby some tea?" Marie asked.

"Sure." These were the first words she'd spoken to me since he arrived.

My mother said, "I'm so sorry. Where is my mind? I should have gotten that for you."

"That's all right," said the professor. "I didn't get thirsty until just now. These greens are delicious."

"Well, there are plenty more. We saved some just for you," my mother said.

Marie's mother asked, "Do you live near here, Professor?"

"Call me Jack, please, Mrs. Hargrove. I live in Hillsboro. But, you know, everything is close around these parts."

Romeo, sitting on a stool near the sink, said, "I like that little town. Didn't Daniel Boone used to live there? Or was it Davy Crockett?"

"I don't know about that," Jack said. He lifted creamed corn to his lips and then looked at Marie sitting across from him. "I should have the class out for a get-together, huh? Have a bonfire or something. Speaking of blazing trails."

Romeo slipped out of the kitchen. I took the trash down the back steps to the dumpster. Down there, I stood with the smokers who sat on lawn chairs in the little patch of yard between the apartment house and the fence that shielded the parking ground. Since the wedding, neither my dad nor Mr. Hargrove had stopped giving me advice on everything from birth control to how to carve a turkey. I hoped for some more advice from them, something useful for the moment. Jack Rigsby could give Marie academic prizes and prestige; what could I give her? Nothing but love. I wondered about Jack's feelings for his absent wife and children. How could he seem so content with that loss?

My father, a big man, stood and clapped me on the shoulder. "Nice party," he said.

"Thanks to Mom," I said.

"You put it together," Mr. Hargrove said. "You young fellows know how to be thoughtful. Brenda is always complaining that I'm not thoughtful. I should do something nice for her, but I can't think of what." He pinched off the burning end of his short cigarette and put the filter into the brown eyeglass case clipped in his checked shirt pocket.

My father said, "You're considered thoughtful if you take your wife on a cruise, buy her diamond earrings, buy her flowers, buy her stuff."

"That's just rich," Mr. Hargrove said.

"I wish Beverly just liked to do what I like to do," my father said. "I wish she liked to fish. If she could learn the beauty of a rainbow trout on a sunny lake, I'd be a happier man."

"Right now," Mr. Hargrove said, "they're all liking that white professor."

"Well, women do like a professor," Dad said. "They like a doctor and they like a soldier. They like a singer, too. I think they like a singer the most."

"Don't forget a preacher. But I was a soldier," Mr. Hargrove said. "I got that at least."

"I can't even claim that," Dad said. "Good thing I'm so good-looking, I guess."

"That professor is kind of good-looking, too." Mr. Hargrove looked at me and laughed a little. "He can't sing, can he?"

"I hope not," I said.

They both laughed. My father said, "You get all the points today, son. When you were born, your mother acted like she was in love with her obstetrician—all for delivering you safely. Hugging him big time every time she saw him. Gushing about how he saved you. You had that cord around your neck, you know. Even your first name is his last name. That's a coincidence, sort of, but one she values a lot. Made me jealous. But she never forgot how you really got to be, if you know what I mean." He winked at Mr. Hargrove, then arched his brows at me.

"Thanks, Dad, I think," I said.

Mr. Hargrove said, "It's always strange when a white man is in the house."

"That OB is black," Dad said. "If that's what you're getting at."

"You know what I'm getting at," Mr. Hargrove said.

Then I thought about my talk with Marie the night before. I hadn't had a chance yet to talk with Dad about possibly changing jobs, and I wondered if he'd ever faced similar disapproval from Mom. He was half-retired from managing the house of a wealthy white family. He'd started as a chauffeur, driving their kids to and from school when they were young, but then started seeing to the gardeners and the general maintenance of the house. I knew Mom used to resent the time he spent with that family. He even went on vacations with them, to their beach and mountain homes. But had she belittled him for the work? Maybe. I didn't want to ask about it now in front of Mr. Hargrove, who owned a gas station. I'd once gotten in a fight with a kid who called my dad a "house slave." And Dad did used to seem a little too proud of coming home in his boss's new station wagon or Cadillac. I used to resent his boss's kids that he drove around in those cars. I wasn't planning on serving white people indefinitely. Marie needed to give me a break.

Inside, the professor was eating coconut cake. I had thought we were saving that for when Marie opened her gifts, when we would sing "Happy Birthday." I kept going in and out of the kitchen, cutting my eye at Marie, who looked at me blandly as I passed. Maybe she at least wondered what I was doing. I was seeing to the other guests, making sure the old folks had something to drink. And I was trying to seem interested in what Jack Rigsby had to say. Trying to share Marie's appreciation for him.

In the bedroom, I found Romeo eating cake with Marie's girlfriends. All three sat on the bed. Ballroom dancing was on the television. "Ray," he said. "Tell these ladies that I'm the king of the tango."

"No, don't tell us," one of the girls said. This was Karen, whom I didn't like much. But Marie had known her since kindergarten. At our rehearsal dinner, she asked me what gave me the most pleasure of all the arts, and I said music. "See?" she said to Marie. "Guys his age always say music." She was skinny and chinless and probably envious, trying to instigate something.

"You tango?" I asked Romeo.

"I do," Romeo said. "Do you?" he asked the girls.

"I do not," Karen said.

The other, Lena, another childhood friend, leaned into him. "You look like a mambo man to me."

"Mambo, yes. And I can teach you to tango as I learned it in Buenos Aires. It's more than teaching you to dance. It's teaching you to be danced."

Karen rolled her eyes. Lena said, "Do I really have to be helpless?"

"No," Romeo said. "You have to be trusting."

I left Romeo to his audience.

In the living room, two old women sat on the sofa with plates of cake on their laps. They were Mrs. Jenkins and Mrs. Clay. Their husbands sat opposite them on scavenged chairs. Mrs. Clay's eyeglasses were so smudged I doubted she could see who I was. Along with some other gifts, Marie's present from her professor was still on the coffee table in front of them. It was wrapped in shiny blue paper and shaped like a pen and pencil set, but it could have been something more personal, like a bracelet or a necklace. It was hard to know what a professor would think was appropriate for his favorite student, as if giving her the outstanding achievement award wasn't enough.

"How would you like to hear some music?" I asked the old ladies.

"Oh, that would be nice," Mrs. Jenkins said.

"Sure would. Nice," said Mrs. Clay.

I knelt at the bookcase before the shelf of records and found the Donny Hathaway LP. If women liked a singer, then I could give them one. As I slipped the record from its sleeve, my dream of the night before came back to me. I forgot I had dreamed it. I had been standing on the dark interior staircase of my high school, crying. It was a variation of a recurring dream I had had since I met Marie. I would be at school in the lunch room, in the media center, on the grounds, on the stairs, looking for her, feeling confused about whether or not she was even a student at the school, panicking in aggravated expectation. But in the last dream, I wasn't afraid. I was on the stairs crying so hard water flooded the stairwell.

Donny Hathaway's voice sounded extraordinarily soulful, and both sealed and soothed that dreamed grief. I smiled at the old women eating their cake and they nodded their approval of the music.

I went to the bathroom to be alone a moment, to take a breath for the rest of the day. But I walked in on Romeo, who was sniffing the tip of a fingernail file. "Shit," he said, flashing his smile, "doesn't that lock work?"

"Jesus, Romeo. What are you doing?" I shut the door fast and locked it right.

"Smack. Want some?" He held out a small bag of white powder.

"No. Thanks. That's heroin?"

"Yeah. Just a snort. I wouldn't shoot it in your bathroom, man. You look like you could use some. Mellow you out. Take your mind off how boring your party is. No offense, man. I know it has to be this way. But all these old folks and that white dude—even those chicks in there are lame."

"Anybody could have caught you, Romeo. Marie would have a fit."

"It's cool, Ray. Only you caught me." He laughed. "Sorry about the lock, though." He closed the bag and put away the nail file. He wiped his nose. "All right. I'm grabbing another brew, then."

After he left I rinsed the sink and splashed water on my face. My face felt a little numb. I'd already had one beer too many. I needed to finish the party. Christ, I didn't know Romeo was into heroin.

I hollered down the back steps for Dad and Mr. Hargrove to come in. I gathered everybody in the living room and sat Marie on the sofa between the old ladies, and my father and I made sure everybody had a glass of champagne. Romeo held a beer in one hand and his champagne glass in the other. He was grinning, showing his dazzling teeth.

"You have a beautiful face," he said to Marie. She blushed with embarrassment, but then held her face up and grinned back at him.

I made a toast to my darling wife, wishing her a happy birthday, and predicted for her a brilliantly successful medical career. Then her father said some words about his pride in her, and grew teary-eyed as he recalled what she had overcome already, her illness, and what she still had to overcome. I took that last as a reference to her being married at so young an age, to me. But maybe he just meant finishing college, getting into med school, becoming a doctor. He and I got along all right. I lifted my camera and snapped a shot of her beaming at him.

Then the professor raised his glass. "Marie is a fresh breeze among students," he said. "Her insatiable curiosity, impeccable preparedness, and beautiful spirit make her a bona fide star. And like you, Ray, I predict superb things for her."

"Hear, hear!" my dad said.

In the background, under the spattered applause, Donny Hathaway began singing "To Be Young, Gifted and Black" softly and reverently. Marie opened her presents and held them up for the room to see and exclaim over. Her friends Lena and Karen gathered up the wrapping paper as Marie ripped it from the boxes.

It seemed odd hearing that special song with Professor Rigsby in the room. While I didn't want him to feel excluded, it made him seem all the more like an intrusion. But I was glad it was playing now. The timing was perfect, as I had wanted to play it for Marie, who was all of the things the song was about. She smiled at me, which took me by surprise. She was happy, and I was glad I'd planned the party. She opened the professor's gift, a pen and pencil set made of sleek wood with her name engraved on the sides, and she looked at him with the softest expression of appreciation I could imagine. It was an expression that he mirrored. Suddenly I felt as if I were dreaming awake. I felt prophetic. I felt the ache of our future. I could hear her say, *Ray, we need to talk; this was a mistake, and you know it. After all, what did we really have in common?* She wanted a professor or a banker or a physician, and I didn't have faith that I'd ever be other than a waiter. Yet for the moment I had something going for me. I was celebrated too by the song. I was certainly young and certainly black. And I felt I had the greatest gift in Marie.

Beauty

RAY STOOD BY THE SERVICE DOOR WATCHING THE GUESTS ARRIVE in formal wear. His staff—fifteen men and women—posed along the walls in white waistcoats. They looked nearly military. Since the afternoon setup, he'd felt a little outside himself, as he often did. Sometimes, for instance, he might neglect to speak when spoken to. Instead, he waited for the self he was observing to speak. It was like two days ago when Professor Green, Ray's former college teacher, introduced him to Alma. And Alma had quickened his heart.

They were lunching with a group at the hotel's main floor restaurant. Ray had finished a breakfast meeting in one of the small conference rooms. While his staff broke it down he roamed about. Dr. Green noticed him, waved him over to the all-you-can-eat buffet.

He observed Professor Green's introduction of Alma Rind: from Florida, where she was all-but-dissertation in library science at the University of Tampa, in town to interview for a university job. When Alma held out her hand, he took it, smiled. Her face was narrow, her mouth large, eyes brown and bright. Big straight teeth. Long full lips shined with transparent gloss. "Hello," said the mouth, cool and friendly. "How are you?" She looked familiar, maybe someone he'd wished for, or a composite of such people.

He thought to say "fine" and he thought to say "good." He said "food." She laughed. She didn't know, or didn't believe, the effect of her beauty, which, he could see, was nearly not beauty at all. Insinuating features, outsized, the longish nose. But the eyes and smile, the voice, the bones of her wrists, the slender shoulders, the long leaning neck, were beautiful.

"Pleased to meet you," he said, chuckling, and glanced around the bright room. Dr. Green, sixtyish, with green eyes, said she hoped to lure Alma's intelligence and energy. She said Ray could vouch for the campus harmony. He'd had a crush on Dr. Green, her ironic eyes, her short skirts back in the day, her shrewdness. He looked at Alma's plate of broccoli and peas. "Is that all you can eat?" he asked. She laughed again.

This morning, Sunday, she wandered into the banquet room where he unfolded tablecloths over big round tables for eight. It was a large room. "I've been looking for you," she said. "I leave today." He worked under huge brass and crystal chandeliers. His staff wouldn't trickle in until noon.

She had met the campus dignitaries, toured Raleigh-Durham, seen Cary, ridden to Dr. Green's house in Roxboro. She asked his opinion about it all, the region, would she be happy if she were offered the job and took it fresh-out-of-school-almost.

She wore a white blouse and a red-swirled wraparound skirt, the red a few shades brighter than the room's expansive carpet, her hair in glossy braided coils. She had almost no hips or bosom.

"It's changed," he offered. "I'm not sure I know the place. It's as though carpenters came to your house, remodeled, and moved in. You think you're their host, but they think you're their caterer. They'll eat the local food, but then they want something Middle Eastern from takeout."

"Middle Eastern?"

"Or Thai, Mexican, Russian, Ethiopian. Lots of bagels. Prayer rugs. Incense wafting up the hallway. Range Rovers in the drive."

"Yet, the terrain is nothing like Florida."

He unfolded another tablecloth, carefully, as if revealing something. He said, "It's still small enough that it can't hide its flaws. But there are a variety of well-meaning people."

"Rich and poor," she said.

"Right. Boil it down."

"My daddy says everywhere is the same. People and dogs."

Ray moved to another table. Alma took a cloth from a pile on a chair. She flung it so that it snapped open and parachuted onto a tabletop. "I show off," she said.

"You're good at it. But you'll wear yourself out. You'll be too tired to bring out the food."

"I'm bringing out the food?" She carried another cloth to another table and snapped it open, let it float down.

"That is so good-looking." He took in her slender waist, her skinny curves.

"I used to do this for a living. They called me cutie. I never got tired."

That was the way she'd gotten through college. She'd earned a scholarship, then a fellowship, but she liked good clothes, so she worked.

"What about you? Why do you do this?" she asked. She regarded his getup. He was wearing black rubber service shoes, polyester black pants, but a decent white shirt, sleeves rolled. Bowtie clipped to one side of his open collar.

"You're not so cute," he said.

"Oh, all right." She slumped, playing hurt. "I thought I could get that one by you. My skull is too long, isn't it? The way I look, I go from interesting-looking to ugly in a heartbeat."

"You're not ugly enough. I could look at you always. You should agree to marry me right now." He stepped to her and curled his arm around her waist. She arched backward, rolled her eyes upward, stretched her big mouth into a glorious grin. He lifted her and sat her on a table.

"Back to work?" she said. "So soon?"

"We're knotted, now."

"I'm moony, honey."

Then she looked at her watch. "I have to go soon. Taking the 10:30 shuttle."

"What time is your flight?"

"Noonish."

He kissed her, her arms around his neck, her eyes closed, then his.

"So just don't leave," he said. "I can hire you if you don't get the other job. Even if you get it."

"Too generous, Ray. Good kisser, too generous. Sweet as sugar."

"I believe we come true."

"I don't know what you mean."

"Sure you do."

"I have to leave just the same."

"Fine." He backed away from her. She slid off the table. He followed her out to the shuttle. She searched his face. He said, "This," pointing behind them toward the banquet room, "something entirely foreign to what I thought I'd eventually do."

She smiled. "I'm uneasy most of the time," she said.

The shuttle came. His staff arrived. They worked unhurriedly, vacuuming, polishing spoons. Hours later, the tables set, glasses cloudy with ice, they buttoned their coats, waited along the ballroom's walls. Chandeliers sparked with fire. Gleaming guests floated about. He stood apart and watched himself search for that girl.

Second Fire

IT WAS TWO A.M. AND ALMA'S STREET WAS BLOCKED BY FIRE trucks and police cars. Her apartment was in a part of town that suffered from too little off-street parking, so I had to circle widely and park on a dark slope some three streets away. On foot, I huffed the uphill climb, crossed through the traffic blockade. The police cars swung swaths of blue light across the scene, but the fire truck's lights were dark and still. Several people milled about. Things were eerie, including the unusually warm February air. And then I saw Alma on the curb staring up at the house across the street.

My heart began to pound as it had in high school when I would search the campus buildings and yard for a glimpse of Marie, the girl I loved in those days. Back then, I was always filled with expectancy. But with Alma it was different. I thought I would never see again.

She stood beside a tall man who wore a maroon bathrobe and a yellow nightcap shaped like a windsock. The man swigged from a bottle of beer. At his slippered feet were two nearly complete six-packs. Alma held a two-liter bottle of Dr. Pepper in one hand, and with the other she held a cell phone to her ear. Her gray sweatshirt came to mid-thigh on her black leggings, and the untied laces of her laser-white sneakers dragged the ground.

"Alma?" I said.

She and the man turned to look at me. She reached to hug me with the arm that held the drink and put her cheek to mine. Her other cheek still occupied the phone. Her headgear was a striped silk scarf, the multicolors muted and altered by the swirl of blue and dim light. A tough little braid poked from beneath the scarf and bristled against my forehead.

"Ray's here," she said. "My friend. I'm glad you're here. I'll be *fine.*" She looked at me, the curb, then back at me. "This is a mess." I understood that she was talking to both me and the person on the phone. I followed her eyes and the pitch of her voice to guess when I was the primary audience. That helped my heart to quiet.

Firemen tramped past in big boots and baggy stiff pants to the fire trucks and to the house. Some wore their long, heavy, reflective coats open and some, without coats, showed wide suspenders over their T-shirts. From the bottom floor of the house, they flung dark, wet lumps out of the gaping windows and doorway. It was a three-story house. A couple of college-age guys, not firemen, toed some of the lumps in the small yard.

Alma paced along the sidewalk among other people standing around. I asked the man with the beer, "Do you live here?"

"At the top." He pointed. "I was the last to know."

The top floor looked like a turret, a windowed cap set upon the cube-shaped house. But only the bottom floor seemed damaged by the fire, although firemen came and went from all the floors, scuttling down the metal steps on the side of the house, entering and exiting the main door in the center. The neighboring houses were large, too, sectioned into apartments it seemed. The few people looking on from those yards didn't look like families.

Alma moved to my side again. "This is Wendell," she said. Did she mean the person on the phone or the guy in the robe? The man in the robe pointed to himself.

"Want a beer?" he asked me.

"Thanks." I stooped to the six-packs at his feet. Light and shadow played along the glass bottlenecks like the activity of another little world. Wendell's slippers were black velvet with red and gold embroidered crests. Tattoos curled amid the hair along his white ankles.

I stood and took the cap off my bottle. "How bad is it?" I asked him.

"Those dudes got the trouble." He tilted his bottle toward the two college-age boys searching debris in the yard. "The fire started in their place on the first floor."

That meant Alma was on the second floor, unless she lived in the turret with Wendell. I looked to her, still on the phone, and asked, "What's the situation here?"

She smiled slowly, distracted. Then she frowned. She waved her arm at the scene, palm up. Are you blind? she seemed to ask. Then, "All right. Bye. I'll call you." Which is what she had said to me a year ago, that day at the hotel, as she boarded the airport shuttle going back home to Florida after her job interview. That was the last time I saw her, or heard from her. I had known her for two days. When she kissed me that day in the Pine Room, me in my waist-length waiter's jacket, could it have been just for fun? Was it a gratuity for me and nothing for her?

One of the firemen, a man in full gear with gray hair showing under his tilted-back hat, reported that the fire was out, that they could return to the second and third floors, but that they probably wouldn't want to spend the night there. "It smells pretty smoky," he said.

The fireman walked across the street to talk to the college boys. They looked at the broken windows of their apartment, scorched sections and soot darkening the shutters and planks around that wounded space.

"You can stay at my place," I told Alma. I wanted to ask now what had happened to her, why she hadn't communicated in the year since I'd met her. I hadn't even known she was in town, in residence. Apparently she had taken the job she interviewed for, a conclusion I drew when she phoned a half hour ago and told me her apartment was on fire, then gave me the address.

"Wendell? You got somewhere?" I asked. "And how about those guys?" I had a sleeping bag and blankets. People could sleep on the couch and the floor. Alma could have the bed. I had to be at work in a few hours anyway.

"I have a friend next door," Wendell said. "He gets off work about now and should be home in a little while. He's a bouncer," he continued, as if to explain the late hours.

Alma said, "Those guys have parents in town. Already called." She gave the cell phone to Wendell, who dropped it into the pocket of his robe.

"Slow parents," I said.

"Slow boys," Wendell said.

I said, "Why'd you just save beverages?"

"I was thirsty," Wendell said.

"Me too," said Alma. "Must have been the heat."

Alma followed me home to East Durham. I washed the smoke-scented clothes she had stuffed into a smoke-scented suitcase when the fireman let her back into her apartment. I had a box of under-sized toothbrushes, still in cellophane. I had a box of small black combs. I had shampoo, conditioner, and skin lotion in bottles the size of chess pieces, the perks of doing business with the hotel. Plus, there were shower caps, disposable razors, soap, and sewing kits. So much to give, I thought, as I set out on the bathroom sink the little things I thought she might need.

Alma decided she would skip work the next day. She had taken the library job after all—of course. She phoned her office and left a voicemail, explaining about the fire. Then, after a brief contest about where she would sleep, on the bed or the pullout couch, she accepted the bed. I set out some cheese and crackers, poured her a shot of whiskey. It was already four a.m. She looked tired. I needed to be at work at six to set up for a breakfast and a brunch. I stood in the doorway of my bedroom and watched as she nibbled a cracker and sipped the whiskey.

"Did you get my letters?" I asked. "Or maybe I had the wrong address."

"I got them. Very nice letters." She ran her hand over her head, slipped off the scarf and jostled her firm, fuzzy hair.

"Well what happened?"

"Well, I'm sorry. I was going to answer. To call you. Maybe. I couldn't decide."

"Why not?"

Her frown made me feel bad for asking. She'd been displaced in the middle of the night by fire. She had called me for help when she needed it. Why not let her rest? Why bother her about her absolute silence, her bewildering discourtesy, her success at making me feel foolish and doubtful?

She said, "I didn't want to be locked into anything before I even moved here. They offered me the job, and I thought about it awhile, and I decided finally that I'd get here, get situated, get the feel of things, meet some people, and then I'd contact you."

"Maybe."

"Well, I have. And I'm glad. And I'm grateful you wrote to me and came to help me. My mother thanks you too, for helping me. She was on the phone when you got there. I don't know what I was thinking before, really. I mean, why should I have been trying *not* to have a friend?" She had on a long-sleeved T-shirt I'd offered her and her leggings. Her sneakers were on the floor by her bare feet. Her hands rested in her lap.

"You must have thought I was in love with you or something,"
I said.

She smiled and shook her head.

"I don't know," I said. "What you said makes some sense. I wish
you'd said it months ago."

"Me too. You were out of sight, and I was out of my mind, I
guess. I get depressed, see. And I forgot you were this real."

"Yeah, well, I know what that's like. I got the same suspicion
about you."

I left her alone to sleep. After I showered, I made coffee while the
muted rap bass swelled from the paper man's car. I heard the paper
thump the ground and listened for the bass and the whining trans-
mission to fade before I ventured outside. For some reason, the
deliveryman drove down the street in reverse. Whine-stop, whine-
stop. And then a long diminishing whine as the car went elsewhere
on the route.

By all appearances it was still nighttime. The warm air was humid.
I sat on my brick stoop and scanned the paper under the yellowish
porch light. News of the president, wars, car crashes. A bank collapse,
a union strike, an epidemic. None of it really interested me, except
to set me to considering that so much of the world went on beneath
my awareness—apparently not happening one day, and then front-
page news the next. Everything thoroughly beyond my control. One
of my waitresses, the Buddhist, sometimes talked to me about cause
and effect, and holding the newspaper I wondered now about all the
latent effects simmering somewhere in the universe. What were their
phenomena before they manifested? They lived as light, maybe, like
the light on the bottlenecks of Wendell's beer, alive on the edges of
things, gleaming, hardly noticed, waiting to erupt into full-blown con-
sequences. Bomb blasts. Or they lived like fire lurking to ignite. They
existed as signals along lines and airwaves that resulted in a ringing

phone, or as mysteries such as Alma's mind. What had caused her to forget me for months and then to think of me tonight?

The neighboring houses were dark, as they usually were at this hour. It was a little after five now. Before heading out to the Research Triangle, I drove back to Alma's street to check on the house in the gradual light. Fire trucks still blocked the street. While I could park closer, I had to walk some before I saw renewed activity at her building. The fire had restarted, and though it seemed out again, the building was all but destroyed. One corner of the roof was burned away. The gray siding around Alma's front windows was charred, and a section of a side wall was blown out. The front of the bottom apartment was blackened and thinned to skeleton. Wendell's turret seemed intact, except for broken windows.

I saw Wendell at the curb across the street again, along with the two boys who lived on the bottom floor. The boys seemed near tears. Their fathers, men in Izod shirts and golf jackets, stood by them. Wendell had on a red dashiki and overalls, and the velvet slippers. Nobody had known how to contact Alma, I guess.

"I missed the main event," I said to Wendell.

"I think Alma's kitchen exploded," he said. "After you left. It was like a rocket's tail flaming out the side. The fire trucks had gone. Everything was quiet. I had finally fallen asleep, and then *boom*! Next door, the fire was so close. I thought the whole block would flame up."

"But people are okay?"

"Fine, man. I just hope my stuff is salvageable. Maybe nothing burned up there 'cause the fire folks got here, but all the smoke and water, man. Poor Alma. Where is she?"

"I need to call her. Let her know."

Wendell pulled his phone from a breast pocket. Blue tattoos swirled under his shirtsleeve and looped around his wrist. Under the brown hair on his chest green leaves sprouted from a vine.

"Not now," I said. "She's sleeping."

"I wish I was," Wendell said.

The yard was covered with wet, blackened things from the house and flattened hoses from the fire trucks. There were books, rugs, sofa cushions, and things too piled upon and altered to recognize. A policeman approached the college boys, who tucked themselves closer to their fathers. Maybe they were in trouble.

Two fires, I thought, as I drove away from Alma's neighborhood, and I hadn't seen a single flame. I decided I would call Alma from work, but not immediately. I'd call between the breakfast and the brunch I had to serve today, as long as I reached her before she left the house. There was no telling what she had lost in the fire, or how she would react. I was curious to find out. But for a couple of hours at least, I reasoned, it was fine not to know. Alma could be kept in the dark.

At about ten I called Alma to tell her about the second fire. She wouldn't answer my phone so I had to wait to call out for her once the answering machine picked up. Just more awkwardness to an awkward task. I tried to explain that it looked bad this time but that I didn't know for sure. I promised to meet her at her apartment as soon as I could, after the brunch I had to serve. She was silent, and then gave a heavy sigh. "Shit," she said.

When I arrived, the fire trucks were gone. The temperature was still disturbingly warm. A very crazy February. A few people I didn't recognize seemed busy in the front yard. One man in headphones moved slowly through the debris as if looking for something. A woman sat on the front stoop cleaning photographs by dipping a cloth into a cup of water and slowly rubbing away soot. She looked up at me and smiled. "Are you Ray? Alma's upstairs." She pointed through the dark front door. I entered, wondering if it was safe to be inside the house. The stairway was black. The carpeted stairs were sodden with water and soot. The air was so dense with the smell of smoke and ash, it was as if I were climbing inside a chimney. As I neared the second landing, I had to look behind me to see any light. It seemed to enter and die at the front door. The way ahead was pitch black. I crept slowly, trusting there'd be a floor beneath my next step, and a lighted destination.

Finally there was dark gray light. It came through a sooty, glass-paned door that was half open. I called for Alma, feeling a little as I had on the phone that morning, calling her name into a space where she possibly wasn't, where she possibly wouldn't hear. I didn't venture beyond the door. It took a moment for the forms inside the room to gain shape, all covered with soot, but seemingly unaltered by flames—a couch and chairs, tables and lamps, as uniformly black as if made of judges' robes. "Alma?" I called, and with a shock remembered the day I looked for Marie at her house, the day she wasn't there. I had called through a dark doorway then and been frightened by the nothing that was there. "Alma!" I called again.

"I'm back here," came her muted reply. I ventured past the glass door onto a floor of mud. Thin mud, it turned out. Books and other, unrecognizable lumps floated in it. Wading carefully, I heard her say, "Avoid the kitchen." I stopped at the kitchen doorway on my left and peered in. A hole in the opposite wall looked out on the house next door. There was a hole in the floor, too, that offered a view of darkness below. The kitchen was toast. Charcoal.

I found Alma in a bedroom, which was less damaged than either the kitchen or the living room. I could make out colors in the bedspread and the brown wood of the furniture. Alma was emptying clothes from the dresser drawers into large green plastic bags. Four bags already bulged beside the bed.

"Alma. I'm so sorry. How are you?"

"Better than a couple of hours ago. Maybe some of this stuff I can keep."

"I can help do something. I have the rest of the day."

She stood looking into the opened drawer and didn't say anything.

"How about these?" I said, indicating the full bags. She nodded. I picked up one and hauled it out of the apartment. For a while, I took out bags as she filled them, and put them in the trunk of my car. I hoped she would spend the night at my place again, but I could take the stuff anywhere she wanted it.

I took a break to sit with the woman on the stoop as she wiped the grime off photographs. She had the cleaned ones lined up to dry in the sun along the edge of the stoop. "It's surprising how some of them burned or melted and most of them didn't," she said. "I'm Vanessa. I work with Alma at the library." The man poking about the yard was Wendell's friend. Wendell was upstairs with a crew of people hauling things out of his place. They had rigged up a series of pulleys and ropes, which they used to take down numerous mysterious metal boxes. The man in the yard was using a shovel now, scooping and turning small sections of yard at a time. Along the sidewalk he had placed several CD cases and a small stone gargoyle, a grinning devil with wings.

"That's not Alma's, is it?" I asked Vanessa, pointing out the devil.

Vanessa laughed a little. "That thing's been giving me the creeps," she whispered. "I think it's Wendell's. He lives upstairs." I nodded, said I'd met him last night. "Did you know that he's the Wonderful Wendell? He's a magician and a movie grip."

"Appropriate jobs for a tattooed man," I said.

"These people scurrying around are his assistants of all sorts," Vanessa said. "I don't know what *he's* looking for." Without looking up, she tilted toward the man with the shovel. "Something special, it must be. He's been out here for hours."

A blond woman in a silver station wagon pulled to the curb and lifted a large cardboard box from the backseat. Mistaking Vanessa and me for burned-out residents, she offered us the box, and we promised to make use of its contents, thanking her for her kindness. She cautioned us to share with the man with the shovel and drove away.

"Want some?" I asked the guy.

"What is it?" he said, lifting his headphones. His voice was high, female-like.

It looked like pillows and blankets. "Bedding!" I said.

"Oh. No thanks." And he went back to his diligent work.

"You seem in awe of bedding," Vanessa said.

"I do feel awe at odd times."

Vanessa was of indeterminate race. Mixed race, probably. Or maybe she was Indian. She was dark, with a boyish haircut featuring long black bangs feathered in a slant over her eyes. She had slow, black eyes with very long, feathery lashes. And she had the tiniest diamond studs above her dark, thin top lip at the corner of her mouth, and below her bottom lip, as if she had glittery moles, or as if she had fallen on a ground of diamond dust and gotten tiny hard particles imbedded in her skin. She seemed privately amused, as if behind her slow eyes she was perpetually pleased by how cute she looked.

Alma came out of the dark doorway struggling with one of the garbage bags. She set it down and wiped the back of her hand across her forehead, repositioning a long twist of hair and leaving a smudge of soot. Vanessa and I pointed at it. "What?" she said. She raised her eyes as if she might see it. "I don't care," she said. "This is breakdown time, anyway."

"You'll be all right," Vanessa said. "You have insurance. You didn't die in the fire."

"I wasn't *here*," Alma said, as if it were a regretful technicality instead of enormous good fortune.

"A lady brought this," I said, and showed her the box.

She glanced at it, pulled back the top flaps. "Okay, bring that, too."

We put the bag and box in the backseat of my Volvo since the trunk was full. Vanessa rode back there, too. They wanted veggie burgers, so I got three of them at a drive-thru. Next, Alma wanted a storage unit. Vanessa knew a place that would drop off a big cube at the curb and then pick it up and store it after you filled it with your stuff. That way, Alma wouldn't have to rent a truck. But Alma wanted to see the place.

It was out on highway 70, an orange and blue stucco building backed by a neat line of orange and blue storage pods. The clerk had ruddy skin and a fat wobbly throat, which he clutched every time he spoke. When he wasn't speaking he smoked his cigarette and thumped the ashes in a glass ashtray beside his computer.

Alma settled the details about costs and logistics, and then she told him about the fire, how she would want access to the pod so she could clean the furniture in it.

"It's yours any time of day," he said. "I know about fire. I had a buddy almost get burnt up in a fire. He died but he didn't get all the way burnt up, just his legs up to his knees, so he could still be on view. He fell asleep cooking something on the stove, and they think he probably died of smoke, but the fire trucks didn't get there until his legs were on fire. My brother hated him because my buddy owed him money. We went to see him all laid out before the funeral. My brother slapped him. There was a line of people waiting to slap him. It takes a mean man to slap a dead man. I'm not like my brother." His voice rattled, but it was not mechanically artificial. He had his own larynx. I wondered if his throat hurt. He didn't look well.

"Well," Alma said slowly. She looked to me. I looked at the man. He took a deep pull off the cigarette and drew the smoke down his ugly throat.

"You'll need a hand truck," I told Alma.

"That'll be in there. No extra charge, 'cause of your fire and my sympathy. I'm not at all like my brother. But if you want boxes I have to charge you, 'cause they count them."

Vanessa said, "No boxes. I've got boxes. Let's get out of here."

We said goodbye to the man. Alma thanked him for the hand truck. Vanessa was already in the car when we got there.

"What's wrong with him?" she asked.

"What do you mean?" I asked.

"What do you mean, what do I mean? Why does he keep grabbing that old neck? Why'd he tell us that story?"

"I don't know," I confessed.

"What a horrible man," Vanessa said. "He grabbed his throat as if he thought that's the usual thing people do when they talk."

Alma put on her seatbelt. She said, "Yet he seemed unaffected that we didn't clutch our throats. Anyway, he's better than his brother."

Vanessa sighed and sat back. She folded her arms. "Now what?"

We all seemed at a loss, until Alma said she needed flashlights. "Mines got burnt up," she said in a gruff voice, making a sad clown face.

I had two in my glove box. They worked, and we were at a loss again. We couldn't think of anything more to mock the man behind the counter. None of us seemed to want to go back to her destroyed place.

Alma seemed to be getting down again. Her shoulders slumped and her face was stuck in a blank stare. I said, "Alma, you can stay with me as long as you need to. As long as you want."

"Vanessa," she said, pointing her thumb toward the back. "She has an extra bed. And, you know, propriety and all."

"Propriety? What does that mean?"

"Appropriateness."

"I know what it means. That's not a good reason. I want you to stay where you want, but it is neither inappropriate nor impolite for

you to stay at my place. Unless there is something I don't know. That
could be, of course. You're rather reticent, after all."

"Reticent?" she said. "And that means what?"

"Funny," I said.

"Cut it out, grown-ups," Vanessa said.

I started the car.

"You need cleaning supplies," Vanessa said.

I headed for a store where we got a bucket, three gallons of water,
some detergents, and sponges.

Back at the scene of the sullied house, Wendell's friend was still slowly shoveling the yard. It seemed the other assistants had left. Alma
scanned the recovered items along the curb and found many of her
CDs and her Monte Blanc pen. Some of the CD covers were melted,
but the disks inside were in good shape. These discoveries cheered
her. "Keep up the good work," she said to the man. "And I will as-
cend to my devastation." Wearing the headphones, he smiled at her.
Vanessa resumed cleaning photographs.

Despite the warm weather, the February light was fading. Alma
and I shone flashlights at her uncertain vases and furniture. The light
seemed to pick out nothing distinct—a gleam in a mirror or other in-
completely smothered surfaces. It was too oppressive in there. But we
bagged lamps from her end tables, knick-knacks from her mantle, her
framed and unframed paintings from the walls, where their absence
left negative shadows—white rectangles. "Your books are ruined," I
said. We bagged more from her closets, stuff from her bathroom, and
left the bags for the next day when we would load the storage pod. I
took for granted that I would help. I had already planned to let one of
my veteran waiters lead the lunch service tomorrow. That's all we had
for the day, and I could go in tonight to make sure the setup was done.

We joined Vanessa on the front stoop in the rapidly waning daylight. I looked at some of the snapshots she had worked on. Alma posed in some with straightened hair, some on the beach, with people who could have been her parents, and with utter strangers to me. Beside me, she sat with her hands between her knees and didn't narrate the images. Instead she wondered aloud what the man with the shovel was looking for. What small thing was so important?

"Maybe it's a computer disk," Vanessa said. "Something with all of the magician's tricks on it."

"Vanessa, you're very psychic," Alma said.

"Really?"

Vanessa looked at me slowly, the long lashes lifting slightly. I wondered if her faint smile now was from her private psychic knowledge.

I said, "Maybe it's a notebook of payouts from blackmailed movie stars."

"What was in all those metal boxes he moved out?" Alma asked.

"Money," Vanessa said.

"That guy is looking for a disk of encrypted bank account numbers," I said.

"He's looking for a sorcerer's stone," Vanessa said.

"They've lost a magic ring."

"Crystal balls."

"Those were shrunken heads in those metal boxes."

Alma said, "I read somewhere that the two most embarrassing states of existence are being ignorant and being unloved."

"What's that got to do with anything?" Vanessa said. "Oh, I know."

"Well," I said, "*I'm* embarrassed."

"In life the embarrassment is to be ignorant. In death it's to be unloved."

We pondered that a while. The man had progressed almost to the other end of the yard. His shovel made wet scraping sounds as it slipped under layers of muck.

"You're better than your brother, right?" Alma asked.

"I don't have a brother," I said.

"I don't either," she said.

"I know that, Alma. You told me about your family when we met."

"Right. Wasn't sure you remembered."

"I have two brothers," Vanessa said. "Nobody's better than they are."

Alma began gathering the pictures from the edge of the stoop. She'd be going off to Vanessa's and I'd be going back home alone with her bags in my car. I didn't know what she wanted me to do with them—take them into my house, bring them to Vanessa's, or put them in the pod tomorrow. All day, being with her, I had staved off the feeling of being a chump, but now I was sinking into it. We walked away from the house and gestured goodbye to the guy in the yard. "Goodnight, Vanessa," I said. I gave Alma a little parting salute.

She leaned into me, grinning. "Don't worry," she said. "I won't slap you when you're dead."

"You'd better not," I said, and walked to my car.

Inside, belted up, I felt pressed upon by the crowded backseat. I pulled forward, watching in the rearview mirror as Vanessa and Alma went the other way. I'm not dead yet, I thought. I rolled down the window to feel the warm breeze of the strange, disorienting weather.

Wave

Sometimes because of traffic Ray cut through a neighborhood that emptied out behind the hotel where he worked. He
operated a waitstaff service that was contracted to a small hotel in
Research Triangle Park. It was a quiet street, twenty miles per hour,
though fairly busy just before school in the mornings and in the afternoons when school got out. At one house about halfway in, there
was a man who sat on his porch and waved. The man waved no
matter who was passing by. He waved every time, at every car, at everybody. He was always on the porch, unless the weather was bad,
and then he sat on a stool inside the glass storm door and waved.

Ray had recently discovered this alternate route, finally found a
way around the clogged stretch of expressway. Lately the usual wrecks
and congestion were caused by sandbags in the lanes, and chick-
ens, lumber, or wet paint. The oddities seemed to compete, to Ray's
amusement and frustration. There had been roofing shingles, cats,
loaves of bread, golf balls, and a washing machine blocking the way.
The hazards of the economy. So Ray needed the shortcut. After the
first two greetings from the man, when Ray realized the man was not
simply friendly but somehow stunned into a compulsion to wave, his
dilemma was whether or not to wave back. If he was in a rush, Ray
sometimes noticed too late and threw up his hand at the neighbor's

porch, as if his wave might trail backward like a ribbon and flutter at the man before snapping forward to catch up. He felt silly waving to a possible idiot. It made Ray feel like an idiot, making an empty gesture at an empty-headed old white man who waved because he couldn't help it. It was like talking to a doll. He couldn't fully pretend it was meaningful. Yet if he did not wave he felt guilty. Sometimes, traffic or no, he stayed on the main road to the front of the hotel, only to chastise himself for preferring the stress of traffic to the stress of waving.

Occasionally, policemen pulled over cars for exceeding the street's speed limit, drivers late for school or work, or maybe rushing because of fear of the waving man. The man's house was small and blue, with a neat little yard. Azalea bushes trimmed the border along the porch. A clean concrete walkway led to three porch steps. The porch was fenced by a painted wooden rail, and behind it the man sat in a rocking chair and waved. He was a big man, as chubby as an infant, with an infant's bald head and dimpled smile. He had gleaming small teeth and silver-rimmed glasses. In cool weather he wore a dove-gray cardigan, and when the temperature was warm he wore pressed pale-colored sport shirts. He was neat, clean, with plump, soft-looking hands. Sometimes he leaned forward from his chair and waved. When he was behind the glass door, as he was this morning, and Ray had to make an effort to find him, the man would also be ducking and leaning in an effort to be seen.

Desperate optimism, Ray thought. This on a bleak, wet, early March morning when, the rainy night before, Ray had discovered someone lying drunk and crying in his backyard, trapped in the narrow space between his back hedges and rusting chain-link fence. Hearing the cry, Ray had gone out in the downpour and aimed a flashlight on him, a ruddy-looking man with soaked dark hair streaking his face—some kind of Indian maybe, in sopping denim shirt and pants, and wearing the weight of wet black cowboy boots. Ray asked if he was all right, what's wrong, tried and failed to pull him up by his limp heavy arm. Shivering, Ray held an umbrella over the man for a while. The man was inordinately sad, eyes closed, speaking no language but despair. Sobbing and moaning. Rhythm and lilt.

So Ray covered him with a blanket and a bunched sheet of blue plastic tarpaulin. Ray's friend Alma was visiting, standing at the opened back door and looking out. She wanted to call the police, or an ambulance. "He'll freeze, catch pneumonia, and die," she pleaded when Ray came inside.

"Catch pneumonia, maybe. He can't freeze out there tonight." He talked Alma into waiting. The police could be more trouble for the man, and an ambulance didn't seem warranted; he was just depressed, breathing well, not hemorrhaging. But they watched the Weather Channel to check the forecast for the night. The temperature would stay in the forties and rain would persist. Then they turned off the kitchen light and stared out the back window, but they couldn't see the man where he lay. He still sobbed loudly now and then, and his intermittent wails reassured them.

Standing there in the dark, sharing a bottle of red wine, was awkward. Alma was not exactly Ray's girlfriend although he had thought she was, or could be. When she first moved to town, months ago, he was all for some romance, and she had a flirty way of being friendly that sustained anticipation. And that night he still hoped for her affection, except the presence of the sad man was an impediment. No way to talk of love, and no sign from her other than her being there. She had come with a betting sheet for the NCAA basketball tournament, wanting Ray's help choosing winners for her office pool. The paper with the names of the hopeful teams in their starting brackets was held by a magnet to his refrigerator, where it semi-glowed in the weak tree-filtered light from a neighbor's back porch. Ray went over and pretended to study it in the near dark.

"Maybe we should take him something to eat, or some coffee," Alma said.

Ray opened the refrigerator and realized the uselessness of taking food out there. "He's not going to eat anything. He's too—disconsolate." He pulled out lunchmeat anyway. And mustard and mayo and lettuce. "Are you hungry?" he asked Alma.

The man outside moaned. "A sandwich would disintegrate in this rain," Ray said.

"Oh I can't bear this," Alma said. "Either that guy goes, or I do. I mean, get him inside or something, which is not exactly what I want while I'm here."

"Well, you're not going anywhere just yet."

"But he's out there like a wounded dog, or deer, or bear. What moans like that? There's nothing human about any of this."

Ray turned to look at her. She was making gestures of frustration and impatience, flexing her fingers and pivoting in her hiking boots, performing in the fan of refrigerator light, her short braids lifting slightly like tentacles.

"I can't put him out of his misery. Besides, a wounded animal is the most dangerous kind, they say."

She stopped pivoting. "You're not making jokes about this, are you? You're using that poor person to make fun of me?"

Ray closed the refrigerator. But Alma was still dimly visible in front of him. "Sorry. It's just a way of being patient, of passing time here. No offense to you or him. I mean, if I were heartbroken and lost, drunk on the ground in the dark rain of somebody's raggedy backyard, I'd want to be left alone. I wouldn't want anybody to know I was even there. I'd want to suffer until I was through without some do-gooder guy and his happy young friend meddling with delusions of rescue."

"Then you ought to shut the hell up instead of moaning and crying to high heaven. And who the hell you calling happy?"

Ray laughed at that. "All right. Damn. Sorry about that, too. I thought you were happy. Why aren't you happy?"

"None of your business." She turned away, and when she turned back, in the semi-darkness, he thought she held her wineglass. There was a glint of light at the position of her heart.

"Aw, you're happy. You're just ashamed to say it."

"If I were happy, you'd know it."

"How?"

She didn't say anything. She raised her glint of light and drank from it. She'd had some troubles he knew about, the job for one—struggling a little bit when she first came to town to be assistant director of special programs at the college library; she was young, just out of grad school. And housing for another—such as having to move suddenly when her apartment building caught fire, and then moving in with a coworker and another roommate who was either on crack or struggling with some alternate reality. That roommate had taken to wearing Alma's clothes and claiming they were hers, that she and Alma had clothes just alike. But all Alma needed to solve the problem was to move again. In with him, would be nice. She could wear *his* clothes. And they could be amused together at what the roommate's disturbance would cause next.

"What would make you happy?"

"I don't have a clue," she said cheerlessly. "Maybe the end of all wars, and all people experiencing personal adoration with humility." She looked down at her wine.

"Of course. Well, that's a clue." Ray stepped over beside her and poured more wine into his glass, and then hers, wishing she would ask him that question. Then he could say that she would make him happy, that he was happy with her just being there, but that holding her would work the magic, having her hold him back. Something real, rather than pretend or cursory like their cheek-to-cheek kisses when they said hello or goodbye.

The man outside was quiet now. Ray flicked on the flashlight and shined it through the window but it was hard to see through the yellow glare on the glass. He raised the window a little to the splatter of rain on the soggy earth.

"Well, it's not good for him to spend the night out there," he said finally, because he imagined water rising up around the man, head in a pool, nostrils filling with puddle and silt.

"Maybe he'll just leave," Alma said. She put her glass down and left the kitchen, went to the bathroom Ray thought.

"There's pretty good drainage out there," he called to her. There had never been any real flooding that he knew about.

Ray took the tournament diagram into the living room, where he sat on the blue sofa and lay the sheet of paper on the glass-topped coffee table. There was light from a chrome floor lamp and the TV was still on, *Animal Planet*—leopards lounging in tall dry grass. He watched that for a few seconds, the image of the man out back swelling onto it. Dry leopard, wet man; if it was meaningful he didn't know how.

For the first round, he picked the teams he knew about but soon understood that filling all the brackets would take some time, some very considered guesses. Everybody picked Duke to win the whole thing, be the team of the decade—the nineties—but the teams Duke would beat were harder to choose. Among them, somewhere, was the team of the '00s. The zeros. Was anybody even hopeful for that distinction, Ray wondered.

Alma came and sat beside him. She turned up the volume and changed the channel to ESPN in case they were analyzing the teams. But it was hockey night, so she muted the sound.

Ray watched her as she went into the kitchen to bring the wine bottle. He said, "Are you hopeful, then?"

"About what?"

"Hopeful. If not happy?"

"Sure." She slid the betting sheet in front of her and took the pencil from Ray's hand.

While she scanned his guesses, Ray thought to tell her about the man who waved, but his mind skipped over to the subject of his boss, the hotel manager who seemed hopeful *and* happy, but was also mean. He was burly, with a British accent and tight suits. He treated Ray like a servant. Ordered him recently, in a room full of his staff, to raise their wages (necessitating some struggle not to offend either his staff or the manager, while trying to disguise his anger and humiliation), threatened to hire another serving group within earshot of customers and staff alike, but then pretended to be friendly, as if he'd been only teasing—such an arrogant, meaty thug, in Ray's opinion. So that was a problem, since Ray's contract was up for renewal. His regular staff depended on him, he thought, and he kept a pool of extras active. This contract kept him steady at the one hotel with pretty good money. He was developing a hate for the manager, but he didn't want to quit.

He wasn't ambitious, he chided himself. At thirty-one, he should have already accomplished more than being a glorified waiter. This week he was to meet with the manager to discuss contract renewal, terms thereof. Still, he wasn't sure he wanted it—another year of that bull. Except the manager might be leaving; he'd heard that from Jamal, the assistant manager, who might take over—a better man altogether. So maybe stick it out—maybe something good could happen—a nice long-term contract eventually and an employer who treated him like an equal, like another boss.

He knew better than to get into all that with Alma. Those thoughts colliding in his head sounded like complaint, like whining, even more so with a brokenhearted man watering the backyard with tears.

So: "Did I tell you about this guy on my way to work who waves at everybody?" he asked. The way it came out, like mockery, even that sounded like complaint.

"No. Something wrong with that?"

"I don't know."

"People wave, don't they? It's a common, person-like gesture." She tucked her braids behind her ears. She had funny ears. They stuck out, even more with the braids pushing behind them. She didn't seem self-conscious in the least. He found that utterly charming, such a pretty, comical face.

"People don't do it like he does. Not like that," Ray said of the waving. "He's automatic, compelled, troubling."

"You don't like him?"

"Yeah, I like him all right. He makes me feel funny, though. It's like he went a little crazy and his mind stuck on friendly, which is better than taking a serial killer turn. Still, while you want to feel good about chronic cheerfulness, it doesn't look any more sane than chronic moping, hatred, and murder."

"Ray," she said, leaning to stare facetiously into his eyes. "What's wrong with you?" She held up her hand and wiggled her fingers in his face.

"What's wrong with *you*?"

"Nothing." She leaned away.

"I want it normal. I want that waving son of a bitch to be sane. He's got somebody inside the house to put a sweater on him when it's cold and to sit him inside when it's freezing and wet, to buy his shirts and to shave him, maybe."

"The Luckiest Man, you mean."

"You got it. One time I was going by and he was helping some lady bring a couple of small suitcases from a car in his driveway—the first time I'd seen him on his feet—and you should have seen the panic on his smiling face. He couldn't wave 'cause of the suitcases, so he just stood there looking at me passing as if I was an ice cream truck coming to flatten him. You know, something both welcome and troubling.

So I waved, and felt perfectly evil then. It was like he was drowning and those suitcases were concrete blocks tied to his wrists."

"Not waving but drowning."

"Well, I guess."

"It's a poem."

"What is?"

"That line. It's from a poem about somebody seeming to wave when actually he's drowning, and somebody else is misreading the gesture. I think that's the reading."

"Oh. Maybe I remember that poem, then. But this guy is just waving. It was like drowning when he couldn't wave."

"You're not evil, Ray," she said, patting his knee. She handed him his wineglass and clinked hers to his. "But speaking of drowning, do you think your boy out back is dead yet?"

"Aw, that guy." Ray glanced back at the dark kitchen window. "What's the matter with him, anyway? How come he gets to do that?"

"He's a drunk man. Desperate. Down on his luck and on the margins of society, lying up against your fence."

"Now you get to make the joke," he said.

He took the flashlight back outside. The rain had eased to a hard drizzle. In the beam of light, rain flashed. The grass was spongy, and Ray stepped over illuminated bare spots of glistening mud. The sound of rain in the trees was enthralling and Ray didn't want to go over to the man. Didn't care to see him lying there passed out or dead, or to hear the sobbing, the thick splat of blunted rain hitting the slick face and wet clothes.

When Ray walked to the hedges by the fence, the man was gone. The light revealed matted grass, flattened tufts of daffodil stems. He pointed the light through the fence in case the man had climbed over and collapsed there. Nothing. Not even a liquor bottle left behind. Alien abduction, perhaps. Alma, he thought, would be relieved.

She left soon after, the betting sheet thoroughly guessed at. Ray put away the sandwich makings, finished the bottle of wine, and fell asleep on the sofa to the hockey game. The next morning going to work he was waving at the man sitting on the stool in the doorway.

It wasn't until after work that he felt bad about the man in his yard again. He had two lunch meetings to serve, and one of his waiters got sick during the shift while another just didn't show up, and still another came in late during the serving with hair limp from rain, her white shirt wet and sticking to her shoulders, which showed pink through the thin fabric. Meanwhile, Ray tried to fill in, going from room to room to keep plates moving, but the hotel manager kept popping in, stupidly commenting on contract points while Ray was hoisting trays of *cordon bleu*, hustling with pots of coffee and pitchers of tea. Then, still short-handed, he had to break down both rooms and set up a larger one for a breakfast meeting tomorrow, check with the kitchen to synchronize the head count because the manager told him late that the number had been increased, and often the kitchen never learned of such changes. While he was there, he had a talk with the dishwasher staff about sending out racks of glasses and cutlery covered with spots that his crew was obliged to wipe away. Then he got on the phone to some of his staff, to leave messages, persuade others to come in very early tomorrow morning to cover the crowd.

Raining all day, a steady, sharp drizzle. Ray had sneaked a couple of moments to stand on the kitchen's loading platform and sip a glass of tea. Then, at five thirty, before leaving for the day, he stood there again and looked out on the lushly wet cedar trees that buffered the hotel from the expressway, and at the stretch of green yard through which the jogging trail coursed. He was tired, yet he imagined the insistent rain excited the earth. Flowers were already springing up, opening. Azalea buds dotted the bushes. Daffodils were already everywhere. He was thinking of Alma, of course, thinking of how romantic the rain could be—the way it encouraged huddling under umbrellas, as it had when he walked her to her car the night before, and the way it sent people indoors with the options of what to do there; he often imagined the intimacy of hotel guests in their rented rooms, and envied them. And then the rain became sad again, gray and relentless, falling all night and all day and probably all night again. He and Alma had done nothing much indoors last night. And the image of the man in his backyard returned. "Forlorn," he said aloud, tasting the sour age of the word. Another little something from a poem. Keats. Alma wasn't the only one with an education.

It was time to go home, the deflated mood of low expectation upon him. Alma wouldn't come by again tonight, two nights in a row, and there was no excuse to go see her and her strange roommate. Surely Alma knew he longed for her, and obviously it didn't matter.

He sat in his car awhile and listened for the traffic report. Incredibly, cattle were loose on the expressway, their transporting truck overturned. The rain slowed a little. Ray circled out of the parking lot and steered onto his alternate route. At a traffic light, he noticed a line of cars behind him, and much of it followed as he turned onto the street through the neighborhood where the waving man lived. He wanted to be alone, not leading a procession through his secret. But maybe it was everybody's secret, and he wondered whether others imagined a relationship with the waving man, too.

It was then, thinking of the waving man, and the sad man still on his mind, that he felt himself held in balance, sustained between his own hope and despair, caught between the waving man and the wailing man. He realized that he was afraid to move, to risk sinking under the weight of his pessimism, or rising up too happy and untethered by solemnity, of being lost in space like the waving man. It was why he wouldn't drive over to Alma's and climb through her window and wait for her in her bed—that and her roommate—and why he wouldn't simply leave her alone. To contemplate either one wobbled him, because for her to accept him would mean giving up his hold on his reality, his suffering, and for her to reject him would send him crashing. It was not a stasis that cheered him.

Maybe, he thought, a similar stasis, a similar fear, kept Alma from being happy. Maybe all it would take was for him to upset this balance, push her off her anchor. And maybe they could soar into a new life, a new decade and new century together. And maybe not.

At the blue house, the man was on his stool behind the storm door and waving. Ray waved back. He looked in his rearview mirror and saw the next driver also wave. The driver was wearing a suit and tie, in a soft-gold Lincoln with green tinted windows. A wealthy man, it seemed, the car old and well-kept, water beading on the polished gold surface like wet jewels. Behind the Lincoln, the wet headlights of the other cars filtered through those green windows, creating a gliding capsule of soft green glimmer, the color of water in the ocean. Ray slowed and kept glancing back to hold the slow float of green headlights, the glimmering green rain on the Lincoln's windows, to ride it around the curves and out beyond the neighborhood to the unobstructed expressway, the wealthy man's car creating a green lens of comfort in the gray day.

On the expressway, the Lincoln pulled around to pass, and Ray waved, thankful for that sustained moment. The man waved back and sped by. Other cars sped by, too, spraying thick rain onto Ray's windshield.

The Naked Eye

BARBARA GAZED OUT THE WINDOW AT DOWNTOWN DURHAM as we drove. It was nearly noon now. "Look," I said, "if this thing takes too long, I'll run and pick up Selena from school and come back to get you. You can handle this by yourself. They won't put you in jail for running a red light."

"I didn't run the light. I told you. The other guy did, and he knows it."

She turned to me and I caught her eye, surprisingly clear and focused. But her indignation was nothing new. My crack-addict cousin had lied to me before. She was even better at lying to herself, and that's what made her convincing.

Barbara had been quiet all morning, nearly serene. Except for a smile when I complimented her outfit, a gray skirt and a pink satin blouse, she'd been blank-faced since I picked her up. Her complexion wasn't good, her thin, pretty face pocked along the jaw and cheek where acne had been badly tended. As I drove us across town to where the traffic records were stored, she licked her dark lips.

We were totally unprepared for court. We needed the police report; we had no lawyer, and Barbara had neglected to get an estimate for fixing her car. Plus, she was still on probation for getting caught with pot. She'd packed lunches for AIDS patients as community service. But at least now we had time to get the police report, because just as we had slid onto the pew-like bench in courtroom 5-D with the crowd of other miscreants, a bailiff told everyone to evacuate because of a bomb threat. He said to come back in an hour and a half.

I didn't know whether to be pissed or pleased about the delay. I'd have to suppress my anger at spending more time with Barbara, not doing what I had planned to do that day, which was to clean out the gutters on my house, rake the yard, and put the leaf bags out on the curb before it rained and got cold again. It was a beautiful January day, Monday, my day off from the hotel restaurant, about sixty-two degrees as we stepped out of the courthouse into the midday sun.

Supposedly, Barbara had stopped smoking crack, so she had Selena again. Although Barbara was prone to partying, when she got busted she claimed that the pot wasn't hers, that she was drug free. Maybe she was.

Of course, Barbara had never really lost Selena because the child lived with her father, who let Barbara see her whenever she wanted. But teachers called Social Services when Selena missed too much school or showed up in the same clothes day after day, her hair poorly combed, sometimes wearing her mother's makeup.

To get off drugs, Barbara got involved with a counseling group at church. There she met bankers and scientists who had lost everything to crack or meth. She seemed impressed by them, and by the few spouses who attended and continued to believe people can change. She still had her job waiting tables at an airport bar. I tried to convince her to come to work for me, but she wouldn't do it, suspecting I just wanted to keep tabs on her. And too proud, I guessed. Four years older than me, she'd always thought of me as her little cousin.

"Barbara, why'd you want me to bring you, anyway?" I asked. "I thought your car was okay to drive." I'd seen the damage, a smashed headlight and fender. The other guy's truck lost the whole bumper and grille.

She kept her gaze out the window. "Because you're a comfort, Ray. Besides, sometimes a woman needs a man just for appearances." She turned to me. "You ashamed to be seen with me?"

"Of course not." She was good at changing the subject, a junkie's skill. Barbara *did* embarrass me. I thought of the rundown heels of her scuffed black pumps and the holes in her dark stockings, which I had glimpsed as we boarded the elevator during the courthouse evacuation. She kind of broke my heart. I figured she had asked me to come so I could pay her fine if she got one. Or maybe she wanted me to see her being responsible, to witness her being vindicated when, for once, the judge ruled in her favor.

Across the street from the traffic records building was a strip mall, and my plan was to pull in there to park. After feeding three dollars into the meter at the courthouse, I didn't want to pay again for parking. Also, I didn't know how much a copy of the report would cost. Barbara should be paying her way, I knew, but I had a feeling that all this nickel-and-diming would be taking nourishment away from Selena. Over the years I had paid Barbara's property taxes, lent her Christmas money, paid off a credit card, and probably financed a pound of drugs, money she never paid back. It was habit for me now. As we neared the mall she said she didn't need me and that if I didn't want to keep her company she could catch the bus back to the courthouse and then get a bus to school to pick up Selena.

Right.

When Barbara was Selena's age, eleven, and I was seven or eight, we used to play jacks behind the couch at her parents' house, when they all lived next door.

Grown-ups would fill the room, listening to records and drinking and talking, and Barbara and I would squeeze between the wall and the couch with our rubber ball and silver jacks, or Old Maid cards, and play. We sat Indian style, and at some point she showed me the white cotton of her underwear, and the new hair growing between her legs. After that, there was no return to the less thrilling bounce and scoop of jacks, especially after she coaxed me to unzip to show myself. We stared. We couldn't wait to do it again. Soon it progressed into a game we called Naked Blind Man. We dared to take off all our clothes behind the couch and to shut our eyes so that we couldn't see each other, or the adults. It was achingly erotic, and also the most trusting experience I've felt, because I never peeked. But we touched, and we never got caught.

I turned to her now. Did she think of those days? Did she wonder what Selena might be doing in private? Our parents had been attentive, drug-free people who kept us fed, cleaned, and dressed for school, warm and comforted at home. Selena could hardly be as innocent as I had been.

A memory surfaced of a less idyllic time when Barbara's father was going to kill her mother—over what, I never knew. My father had to confront him, his own brother, and take away the rifle. Barbara and her mother fled to my house, crying, embarrassed, and scared. I imagined skinny Uncle Lee carrying the gun from room to room, trying to decide whether or not to shoot his fat, sweet wife. As my uncle had clearly gone crazy, I feared that my father might be killed wrestling away the rifle. Barbara and I got behind my couch, without cards or jacks, and let our game begin. I knew I wasn't in love with Barbara, that she was just my playmate. I loved my babysitter, Miriam, and behind my closed lids, I imagined it was Miriam touching me with her clothes off, her warm wet mouth kissing me where I'd never been kissed before. That day held enough fear, humiliation, and pleasure to prepare us for any number of life's awkward moments, including my eventual proposal of marriage to Miriam, which she laughed at.

Once when I was in New Jersey at a restaurant trade show, I visited Barbara in Bayonne. My parents had died and I was just getting my serving business together. Barbara had moved there when she dropped out of Rutgers to try modeling in New York. People always said she should be a model. I stayed with her two days, and that first night we smoked crack together. She didn't call it crack. We were smoking cocaine, is all I knew. It was so sneaky good, so light and teasingly satisfying, that we stayed up until five in the morning chasing it. About midnight, a man came to her door with the deferential demeanor of a beggar, and I understood that he was looking for what we were smoking. He looked as thin as breath and britches, as my mother used to say—oxygen in a sport coat—his eyes large and vacant. So I was not so naïve as to believe what we were doing was safe.

What struck me too were his hands, which had almost freakishly long and splayed fingers. Barbara got rid of him—a callous dismissal. "Go on now, Henry. Get the hell away from here." After he left, she said, "He's a nice guy, but he's strung out to the moon."

"He has prehensile digits," I said. "Like a marmoset."

"Yeah," Barbara said. "He has reprehensible thumbs."

The next day, when I looked forward to more smoke, Barbara provided none, and I knew at least she wasn't hooked. Neither was I. We never talked about that weekend again, as that too felt like a secret, or like something we both had dreamed.

Eight years later, she returned to North Carolina with six-year-old Selena and a husband named Dennis. Her mother was sick with cancer and Barbara tended to her until she died. Her father was already dead. Then Dennis went to jail for selling fake Walmart gift cards, and Barbara divorced him. She worked as a teacher's aide for a couple of years and studied to be certified, but next thing she was entertaining a new group of scroungers at her house until Social Services took her daughter away. Dennis called to say I needed to check on my cousin. He told me Selena was living with him. Somehow the ex-con had conned the state into letting him have custody. That's when I got involved again.

The morning I went to see Barbara was early November, cold and windy. A couple of cars I didn't recognize blocked the driveway. I wasn't comfortable going into the neighborhood because it hurt me to see my old home, next door to Barbara's, with the trees cut down, the garage missing its door and crowded with junk, and the house painted a crude blue, even the metal awnings and the edge of the roof. The view from our porch had been beautiful. As a teenager I used to sit there on summer afternoons and wait for my parents to return from work. The oak and cedar branches spread from thick trunks and made a kind of frame of the yard and the woods and sky beyond the street. But from Barbara's porch that day, the road looked narrower. Prefabricated houses had been put up across the street and completely changed the look of things.

Barbara came to her door wearing sweatpants and a navy sweat-shirt with STRAWBERRY SHORTCAKE fading from the front. She seemed nervous, her eyes tired, bruised-looking. We didn't hug. She led me through the living room, where a twin mattress covered with a thin pink sheet crowded the floor. An army duffel bag sat on top that. The house was cold. In the den she had a visitor, a man in a tan leather coat and matching cowboy boots made of ostrich. He wore a densely patterned silk shirt of gold, orange, and green. Beneath the long bill of a wool cap his dark eyes were ruddy. His beard was coarse and dusty and looked like a clump of bees.

She told the man I was her cousin, but she didn't tell me who he was. We nodded at each other, and he stood and smiled faintly. "'Sup," he said, his island accent strong in that one syllable. I asked Barbara to come back out to the porch, and when she did I told her to get him out of there.

"What? Why?" she said.

"Why not?"

She stared at me, and I sat down on one of the aluminum chairs on the porch. My courage was stronger now that it didn't have to hold me up on my feet. "Does he live here?" I asked.

"No."

"Who does, then?"

"I do. Friends of mine."

"Well, where are they?"

"How the hell do I know? At work, I guess."

"Yeah, right. What kind of work does this guy do?"

"I don't know. What's it to you, Ray? What do you want?"

"Did they move in here before or after Selena left?"

"None of this is your business, man. They pay me. That's what matters."

"Look, tell the dude I'm here on family business and that he has to go now."

She paced the porch floor a few times then went back inside. I took a deep breath and waited. The neighborhood looked desolate. No traffic on the street. No bicycles. No children. I glanced to the left at my old house, where weeds grew up the wall to the tiny kitchen window.

Barbara came back outside with her visitor. She hugged herself and shivered. I couldn't gauge whether the man had showed up and surprised her or she had summoned him. He walked off the porch without saying goodbye and kept going up the street past my old house and out of sight. If he lived in the neighborhood, I wondered where—and when did the neighborhood become home to expatriate Jamaican drug dealers?

"Barbara," I said. "Are you retarded?"

She looked stunned. Then she said, "Why are you being a bitch? You need a cat, Ray. I haven't seen you in a while. What do you want?"

"I want you to act like you've got some sense. How are you living? No wonder you lost Selena."

Hurt and anger tightened her lips. She went back inside.

I followed. We stopped in the den, where the bee-beard man had sat collecting space. She eased down on the low couch where he had been and I sat on the vinyl ottoman across from her. I could see the kitchen, where the sink faucet was dismantled. I noted the sooty fireplace, the space in the bookcase where the TV had been. Old books lined the shelves.

All morning I had been worried about how to handle this, worried about what I'd see when I got there. Barbara still seemed jittery, and I realized she hadn't been afraid of the bee-beard man. She was afraid of me.

I said, "I know you're either high right now or desperate to be so. Either way you're anxious for me to leave, because you know I'm not about to believe anything you say. You need to quit this. You're an addict. All I want to know is, how can you do this to your parents?" I got up and kicked at the curled ash on the hearth. It burst into soft black flakes. "They worked all their lives to be noble, dignified people, and you move back here to kill their good name by running a crack house. If you don't have any respect for yourself, then at least have respect for them. Not to mention your damned daughter."

"My *damned* daughter?" She huffed. "Oh, and for you, too, right?"

"Yes, for me, too. Look. We're both orphans, all right? We're grown, but we're orphans. But I didn't choose to let my folks' values die when they did. We're the only family we have left, except for Selena. I'm supposed to be looking up to you like I always did. How can I look up to you when you're letting everybody down?"

She got up and moved toward the living room. "Stop," I said.

She turned back, slid her hands down the side of her pants as if she expected to find pockets there. "Don't worry about me," she said.

"Everything will be fine. This is just temporary until I get a job, a better one. And get Selena. I'm gonna move then, or first. Meanwhile, you wouldn't believe it, Ray. I'm writing a cartoon. That guy who was here, he does the drawing and he wants me to write the words."

She went to the bookcase and pulled a sheath of papers from atop some books. They were studies of cartoon characters, oddly shaped heads, big eyes, different haircuts and hairstyles, faces with sunglasses and faces on baggy-clothed bodies. They were sketches, nothing to suggest a story or a plan for one, and no words.

"What's it about?" I asked.

"Some kids. We haven't worked that out. We're just working on ideas."

She took the drawings from me and placed them back on the shelf. Then she sat down again and looked at me with a hopeful expression. Was she hoping I'd believe her, or hoping something might come of that cartoon plan?

"Barbara, what makes that guy think you can write a comic strip? Is that what it is? What makes you think you can do it?"

"I'm thinking I could try. Technically, it's not exactly impossible," she said, rolling her eyes. "Hell, Ray, you can see I need a change. I think this could be it."

"How about you try to get off the drugs? What if I contact some places that could help you? What if I helped you?" I felt myself cringing as I said that. I had resisted the idea that this visit would suck me into her shit. Other associations I'd had with druggies had been purely social or circumstantial, and rare—a few old friends, a few transient waiters.

Barbara frowned. She bit the skin of her knuckle. "I don't have time to go inside. I have to work. My unemployment runs out soon. I don't have the money."

"We can work that out. Let's just try."

She did move out for a while, sleeping in a room at a house owned by a man who called himself a prophet. During that time she was renting her house legitimately—or I was, as manager, which earned her some money. The prophet held all-day religious services in the living room of his house, which was furnished with rows of folding chairs and a desk at one end where the prophet spoke. Sometimes Barbara wandered into the living room where, before a sparse congregation, the prophet predicted earthquakes in Asia, bombings in the USA. Eventually, though, she went to the drug counseling sessions I found for her at one of the mega-churches; there, she more or less miraculously learned the error of her ways. It turns out that after her mother died she felt alone in her grief. She simply felt alone. But unlike before, when she responded by getting high with other sufferers, at the church she was with people who found other, cleaner ways to cope.

So Barbara had apparently achieved what many considered the metaphysically possible, emancipation from drug addiction through spiritual intervention. Still, she was a drain on my resources and patience. As I steered into the mall parking lot, Barbara griped about the bus, about how I could just drop her off and go, and I managed to refrain from telling her to shut up.

The strip mall was anchored by a Home Depot and a grocery store, and it housed little restaurants and shops, all of which made for noon-hour traffic in the narrow lanes leading to the parking spaces. I stopped to let a man holding some kind of big orange tool—an orange metal disk with a long handle—cross the lane, and then found a spot a couple of rows from the main street in front of the red-brick records building.

Getting the police report was easy. The woman behind the counter looked heavy and mean, but she turned out to be nice. She called us "dear," smiled with crooked teeth, and didn't charge us anything. We made our way out through a huge ugly gallery where hundreds of drawings and paintings by schoolchildren were on exhibit. Barbara slowed down to look, and I slowed, too, when I saw that some of the work was by students at Selena's middle school. We found sixth-grade work, but nothing signed by Selena.

Outside I asked, "Barbara, didn't you know Selena's class had work in there?"

"I don't know."

"How could you not? Hasn't she talked with you about it?"

Barbara said, "Maybe she doesn't have anything in the damn show. Maybe that's why she didn't talk about it. Ever think of that, Ray? Whoever said Selena could draw a damn picture?"

I took a deep breath. "She can draw. Anybody can draw what's in there," I said, although some of it was pretty good.

Back in the parking lot a police car was blocking my car and a man was talking to the cop through his window. I stepped ahead to snatch an orange flyer off my windshield and to ask the cop to move when the guy started walking toward me, talking. The guy was pointing behind me and I looked but didn't see anything unusual there. When I turned back to him, however, I noticed the big orange tool he'd been carrying attached to the front wheel of my car. He said, "You're booted."

"Ah hell," I said. "You're the guy I let cross in front of me a while ago. You put a boot on my car?"

He held his hands together in prayer position. "I'm sorry, sir. There are signs posted forbidding you to park here for business in the records building. My job is to enforce that restriction."

"You put a boot on my car?" I repeated. His calm added to my outrage. "What signs? What are you talking about? I can't believe you did this after I let you go ahead of me." He pointed behind me again and I looked but still didn't see what he meant. "Where? Where?" I was conscious of the policeman still in his car and realized by then that he was not there to assist anyone in particular. He was there to control the violent.

The boot man walked by me a few steps and finally said with exasperation, "*There*, sir."

I squinted, walked over to him, and saw a row of signs by the street. The red lettering probably did warn against parking; I couldn't make it out. Barbara leaned against my car and held the orange flyer I had dropped, which I now realized was a flyer explaining the boot.

"You asshole," I said. "I did you a favor, and you put a boot on me. You fucking asshole—I didn't see any sign, I saw *you*. I saw you crossing in front of me when I stopped to let you go. You saw me park—why didn't you tell me about the sign? Why didn't you just tell me not to park?"

"Sir, it's not my responsibility to tell you about the sign. The signs are already posted."

"You're telling me about the signs now, jerk. Aren't you? Aren't you?"

"Yes sir, I guess so."

"You freaking, fucking jerk."

"Sir, my supervisor is right over here. You'll need to speak to her."

I turned to the police car. Was the cop his supervisor? "All right," I told the policeman, "how much do I pay you?"

"I beg your pardon?" the cop said tersely. Did he think I was bribing him?

"How much do I *pay* you?"

"No," the boot man said. He gestured beyond the police car to a woman in a blue windbreaker sitting in the passenger seat of a blue Toyota with the door open. I left the policeman.

"Then how much do I pay *you?*" I said to her.

"Fifty dollars," she said, solemn-faced. She had salt-and-pepper dreadlocks. "Cash or credit."

"Fine." I looked over at Barbara. She had her arms crossed, watching me. Staying out of this. The police car pulled away. We had to get back to court. I gave the woman a credit card and watched as she copied the number on a small pad of carbon paper. "Your boy there is an asshole," I said to the lady. "You should put a sign on him, the way he goes back and forth across the traffic."

"I don't have to wear a sign," he said.

I stared at him, paunchy and scruffy in his green cargo pants, Sponge Bob T-shirt, and Cincinnati Reds baseball cap. "You're wearing signs now, bitch. Get the fuck away from me."

I'd never spoken to anyone that way before. I was both ashamed of myself and excited. It felt like a crime of passion, horrible and necessary. Inevitable. By the time the woman gave me the receipt, the boot man was leaving my car, carrying the orange boot. I had to pass him. "Fuck off, fat boy. Hope you drop it on your foot," I said.

He didn't look at me.

In the car I felt a deepening mix of emotions. "Sorry," I said, "but that guy made me mad."

Barbara reached over and squeezed my shoulder.

"I wanted him to feel bad. He set me up. This is about money, otherwise he would have just told me not to park. It's a goddamned racket. And the fact that I'd been nice to him. But I didn't have to call him fat, or a bitch."

"Fuck him," Barbara said.

She had the orange flyer on her lap, covering the police report. I felt another surge of malice. "You can't see to it that your daughter gets in the art show," I said, "so why the hell are you being so careful with that?" I snapped the flyer with the back of my fingers.

She stared at me a few seconds. "Hey, man," she said, "I didn't tell you where to park."

We drove back toward the courthouse, the car so hot now that I pulled off my sweater, unbuttoned the top of my shirt, and rolled up my sleeves. I didn't look at Barbara. Instead, I lowered the windows and tried to calm down. At the courthouse, people were standing around outside, no one allowed in. Barbara and I sat on a bench down the sidewalk from the building, within eyeshot of the crowd so we could see when they started to go inside. I figured I would need to pick up Selena from school and leave Barbara by herself. "Barbara," I said, "don't do anything to get locked up. Just plead no contest."

"No," she said. "I'm not guilty." Then she squinted over at me, smiling. "I love Selena dearly," she said. "And I'm clean. On the straight and narrow. And I love you, Ray, appreciate everything you've done for me. For us. Although it might not be obvious to the naked blind man's eye."

Okay. She'd charmed me with that.

Maybe I had been holding that anger since the bee-beard man, who had frightened me. Or since Barbara took me behind the couch, then grew up and forgot me. Or maybe I'd been holding it forever, since my parents and Barbara's parents, and their parents before them, had worked themselves to lower-middle-class deaths so I could become a glorified servant and she could become a crack addict.

She had her eyes closed in the sunlight and seemed peaceful. The sun brought out the golden-red tone of her skin. Probably the judge would find no fault and consign her to her insurance company. But I didn't relish bringing Selena to her mother at the courthouse. Selena's father had already been in prison; she didn't need to worry that her mother might be next. I wondered how alone Selena felt. Did her friends have ex-con dads and a crackhead mom? And what would be the cost of such misfortune?

I didn't know why Barbara hadn't come to me earlier. I'd lost my parents before she lost hers. She should have known I'd understand her sadness. We were all the family we had left. And though we could hardly acknowledge our memories, they were all that was left of the past.

Luau

MY EX-WIFE MARIE SHOWED UP AT THE LUAU FOR BLACK CARdiologists accompanied by her husband, the black cardiologist Dr. Harry Cushion. I don't mean that to sound mocking. That was the group, that is her husband. He is a broad-shouldered man with receding, tough-looking hair and a patchy, tough-looking beard. He doesn't want a haircut and he doesn't want a shave. He's a natural man. He looks the type to eat raw vegetables for lunch and dinner, to snack on nuts and grapes, the type to brush his big wide smile with baking soda. He's not hard to like, but he's a doctor, and doctors are intimidating for their specialized knowledge, for their comfort with the sight of blood, and for their power. We had a hotel full of them, spilling from the lobby onto the lawn. Candlelit tables and tiki torches cast a gleam on the brown skin of the roasted pig in the freshly dug cooking pit.

Dr. Marie and Dr. Harry—the Drs. Cushion—sat at a table near one of the grass-skirted bars. I went by in my blue Hawaiian shirt, said hello, asked if I could get them anything. I hadn't seen Marie in a long time. A couple of years. But I had seen her husband on television, on the local morning show segment called STAT, where a rotation of local doctors offered tips about high cholesterol, high blood pressure, osteoporosis, breast or prostate cancer. His smile made him telegenic.

He smiled at me now. "Ray," he said. "We thought we might see you here." We shook hands.

Marie stood and hugged me. "Hi, Ray," she said. Her body was strong and softer—specialized knowledge I was pleased to have. "You have quite a large crew here tonight." She looked as great as ever, or somehow better at forty than in her twenties. I sat with them and guiltily considered other knowledge Harry and I might share, the way she used to scoot back against me in bed when she was feeling amorous in the morning. She had a little more to back up with now.

I said, "Lots of folks to be served. Plus, this is our first luau. Everybody wanted to work just to put on these shirts and wear sunglasses at night."

"Yeah, ya'll look cool," she said.

"Thanks. This is a big deal. We don't usually get to work outside, and never with a roasted pig."

"Whose idea was this anyway, Harry?" Marie asked. "A luau sounded fun, but I didn't think about the pig part."

Harry made a dismissive, disgusted face, a grimace sweetened by arched eyebrows. "Wasn't me. The planning committee. Isn't this absurd? We look like we're gathered to eat a cadaver. *Black* cardiologists, of all people, dining on swine."

"Well, you won't be eating any," Marie said to him.

"You got that right."

I touched Harry's skilled hand and then Marie's and excused myself from their table. I was at work, after all. I did have an extra large crew. I had brought back some old talent who had left for better jobs, but who were kind enough or interested enough in extra money to come back and help me for this. And I had hired on new college students recommended by some of my regulars. I had even hired Alma, my girlfriend, for the night. The serving was buffet style, except for a special flaming dessert. But we were helping at the buffet tables, keeping them stocked with mahi mahi, salmon, poi, and mashed sweet potatoes, keeping the dining tables clean, and pouring hot water and coffee for those not into the coconut-and-umbrella drinks.

Alma's job was to give out nylon leis as guests came onto the lawn. Several college girls were doing that, too, some in grass skirts. I wondered if Alma had served Marie and Harry. She and Marie were dressed alike, in flower-patterned halter dresses. That was sort of creepy, and sort of cute. Marie had a pink silk hibiscus in her early graying hair. Alma had a purple orchid headband around her corkscrew twists. I wound through tables and found her near the hotel entrance, the bright amber lobby behind her. She looped a yellow lei around my neck.

"Ah, the coward's color," I said.

"Matches the sails on your shirt. Don't worry," she said. "You're not the only one."

"As expected, my ex-wife and her husband are here. They're so secure. They're both wearing pink."

"The illustrious Drs. Cushion. I should meet them."

"Down front, by the pig, by the bar on the left. Maybe I'll introduce you."

"They're friendly, right?"

"And compassionate."

"Uh-oh."

"No. They're good people. You'll like them. They'll probably like you, too."

Something must have happened to the look on my face because Alma drew closer and kissed me on the cheek. In truth, I was trying to imitate Harry's look about the pig.

"Hey, no kissing at work," I said.

"Relax, boss. This is how we do it on the big island."

A couple in straw hats and striped capri pants approached. While Alma negotiated looping the leis over their hats, I went inside to the bathroom and then went through the kitchen to check on the rhythm of the work. I waved to the chef who was baking the fish. A couple of young waiters came in with empty platters and the chef told them to wait two minutes. I told them to sit down while they could, so they grabbed a couple of stools on wheels and sat resting their elbows on a stainless-steel table.

"How's it going?" I asked.

"I want to be a doctor," one of them said.

I laughed. "Why?" I figured the party seemed pretty deluxe to him, what with the Benzes and Jags in the parking lot. But that was nothing too new for the hotel. But to see so many successful black people was rare.

He said, "When I was a kid I saw a man with big fat arms and too-short fingers. Ever since, I have been fascinated by people's hands. How they work. I'll probably be a hand surgeon." He licked his fingertips. His fingers were long and dark with big knuckles.

"You have good hands," I said.

"I know. Why is that?" he said.

"Genes," the other waiter said.

"I guess. I wonder if genes can make me a hand surgeon. If genes can get me through chemistry."

"Fish up," the chef said. And the waiters were back on the move.

I wondered if genes had to do with why I was depressed all of a sudden.

I hung out in the kitchen a little longer, sat down on one of the rolling stools. Of course Marie was the cause. It was strange being friendly when we weren't really friends anymore, after having been married, for however short a time. Over the years, I had phoned her now and again to see how things were going. I was curious about her. We'd been married only two years. It ended before we were settled into our twenties. It was so long ago it was almost as if it had never happened, or had happened to other people. There were things I never learned about her and that she never learned about me. And I wanted to know what had become of the person I had loved when she was young. But on the phone she offered only updates on her career, on her mother and father and other relatives. She had finished medical school, interned in Cincinnati, come back, joined a pediatrics practice, and remarried. The last time I spoke to her, a couple of years ago after seeing her brunching in the hotel with Harry, I called and left a lengthy message, full of questions about her health, her happiness, even about what books she read. Wishful thinking made me stay on the line. She phoned me back about a month later. She left a message saying she had been busy, that she hoped I was well.

Outside, the band was playing. It was a jazz band in tropical gear, pastel linen. Like some of my waiters, they wore sunglasses. The mild rhythm and comforting melody of "Breezin'" lured some couples to the dance area, which was marked off on the lawn in front of the bandstand. None of the couples included Marie, as far I could tell. I picked up a water pitcher and replenished a few glasses as I gazed at the other waiters. The night had taken on a slightly magical quality, with the music enlivening the expansive square of the party and colored paper lanterns strung between poles. Along with the warm smells of food in the warm June air, the flickering candles and colors made me think of the fair when my parents used to take me. I loved the night when the neon and color saturated me and made twirling shapes against the sky. This seemed a more stylish, genteel version of that reckless mood, and I wanted to nourish the feeling that something dizzying might happen. I decided to let Marie have her good time. I'd try to share this anticipation with Alma.

I filled water glasses until I spotted Alma chatting with Ella, one of the serving veterans. I came up to them behind a buffet table. Alma said she had run out of leis. I had resisted the pun all night, so now I cut my eye at Ella, who twisted her pink lips with her fingers, suggesting I button my mouth. A silly enough response to a childish moment.

"What?" Alma said. "You think every horny doc hasn't hit on me already?"

"I'll bet. With your fine self," I said.

"I need a doctor to squeeze my papaya," Ella said, making a fist with each hand. "Sip my guava juice. Macka my damia."

"Pull all the way up," Alma said.

"Sorry," said Ella.

"Any doctor in particular?" I asked.

"None that you know," Ella said. She was aware of Harry and Marie. I had confided in her, as she had in me, during our long association, which had sometimes been quasi-romantic until she got married. I realized I was at an event with three women who had cared for me, and the only discomfort was that I was still heartbroken by the one who had loved me first. Suddenly I didn't know how or why I should introduce Alma to Marie. It had seemed like a casually comic idea earlier, like maybe if I were to drive Alma by my old elementary school to show her where I learned to tell time and to carry a lunch tray. How embarrassing would it be to stand with Alma before Marie and suggest, this is where I learned to pretend feeling like crap doesn't matter?

Despite my yellow lei, I prepared a plate of papaya, pineapple, and strawberries, winked goodbye to Ella, and steered Alma to Marie's table. "We've come to serve you," I said, presenting the fruit, and then I made the introductions.

"Dr. Harry Cushion," Alma said. "What a pleasure to meet you. And you, too," she said to Marie. "Many times I've been tempted to write to this guy to thank him for his commentaries on television. Because of you, sir," she said, looking again at Harry, "I was able to have a particular little problem diagnosed and treated. Your clarity and concern are godsends."

Huh? I thought.

Harry, standing, said, "I'm so happy to hear it. By all means, have a seat."

The horns in the band began to blast something fast and Alma leaned into Harry, presumably to discuss her little problem, whatever it was. I looked to Marie, who was smiling. Then I looked to the pig, where a line of people waited to receive slices of pork. Marie tapped me on the shoulder and indicated the woman toward the back of the line, heavy and pale in sandals and shorts. "She has heels like white elephants," Marie said.

I laughed. "She sure does."

She chuckled. "That's not too mean, is it?"

"I don't think it is, Marie. I think it's the kind of thing I missed about you."

"You shouldn't have missed me much."

This was quicker intimacy than I'd hoped for, this polite disagreement about what I should have felt. "You probably should have missed me more," I said. "But you became so unhappy so quickly, I doubt missing me ever came to mind."

"That was a long time ago. We've both grown up, though. It's nice to see the grown-up Ray."

She was being generous, it seemed, dismissing my complaint, my smarmy aggression.

"I have to tell you that I'm sorry for any contribution my immaturity made to your suffering back then. Whatever I did to make you want out. It was ignorance, and general lack—that's all I can come up with. I wanted you to be happy. And I really wanted to be a part of it."

"Oh, Ray. We do what we do, what we can, with what confronts us."

"All the same, Marie, I can't get over awe at you, for being the same person I loved twenty years ago. I can't get over awe about time, maybe."

She didn't respond to that. She simply nodded. I turned to Alma and Harry and found they were looking at me. I hadn't intended them to hear my sentiments to Marie. Maybe they hadn't. Anyway, this must be how the pig would feel, I thought, if it could feel—on display. I wanted Marie to apologize to me. After all these years I still had no idea what I had done, really, to make her want to leave me, and here I was apologizing for simply being myself, as she acknowledged. But she had hurt me, and she wanted to excuse that with the implication that she had been simply *herself.*

"You know," I said, to do something distracting, "my father died of heart failure. It was a heart attack, really, but heart failure sounds more accurate, since he died. It seems like, if it were an attack, he might have had a chance to fight back. Is there actually a difference? What do hearts do?"

"Ultimately," Harry said, "they fail. And we fail our hearts."

"And my uncle had angina," I said. "Another died of a stroke. They all ate a lot of pork. Pig feet, pig ears, pig knuckles. I'm sure that was a cause."

"No doubt," said Harry.

"My father sometimes got words wrong," I said. "For instance, he'd say 'black Agnes' instead of 'black angus.' My grandmother had spells. I don't know what that was about. I have bad vision and inattention, but I won't wear glasses. Once in a grocery store I was looking for canned meats and went down the condiments and candies aisle by mistake. Same with carrots and crackers. I go to the doctor and forget why I'm there—that my shoulder hurts and my left foot goes numb, for instance. I suspect I'll be lying in bed waiting to O.D. and will have forgotten to swallow the pills."

"Are you being serious, Ray?" Alma asked.

I looked at her serious face. Then I looked at Marie. "You didn't really get to know me. I have a family history of high blood pressure and heart issues. That's just on my father's side. My father's heart was so big they wouldn't let him in the Army." My own heart felt like an empty bucket swinging in a well.

"If only all our hearts were so big," Alma said. "Imagine the state of the world."

"Next time you go to the doctor," Harry said, "tell him all of this. That ought to do the trick."

Alma said, "We'd better get back to work."

Marie asked, "Have you worked with Ray long, Alma?"

"As long as the rose is red, seems like. But this is my first night at the hotel."

"Oh," Marie said.

We all stood. I shook Harry's hand. Marie hugged me lightly. She said, "Sometimes we may think we're through with the past, but sometimes the past keeps things for us to figure out. I got that from a movie," she chuckled. "So don't take me for wise or anything. But it's natural, I think, to want to go back."

I walked Alma back to her station with Ella. "How did that go?" Ella asked.

"That went the way it went," I said.

"Whereupon I came upon," said Alma.

With Ella, we gazed out at the crowd of cardiologists. The band was now playing a hula-inspired melody with a slow bossa nova beat, the guitar mimicking a ukulele. The doctors and their partners waved their arms, making birds and water of their hands and hips. Marie got up among them.

"Dr. Harry is a sensible person. What little problem did he help you with?" I asked Alma.

"I must keep that to myself," she said.

"Okay. Not now, you mean? You'll tell me later?"

"Maybe. Geez, Ray. It's personal."

No one was telling me anything I needed to hear. I said, "The things I don't understand are as wide as the world."

Ella said, "*Each* thing I don't understand is as wide as the world."

I said, "Most things I don't understand can't even fit into the world."

Alma said, "Some things I don't understand don't even exist yet."

I pondered that. She had a gift for near and certain nonsense. "Alma," I said. "Thank you. That's very oddly helpful."

Vacation

I GOT TO DEXTER'S HOUSE ABOUT SIX ON A WARM OCTOBER Saturday evening. His wife Olivia opened the door wearing red capri pants that looked new and a white T-shirt and red sandals. She looked like summer and Christmas at the same time, but as I said, it was fall. She carried two shopping bags and clutched her keys in the hand that held her red purse. I couldn't tell if she was coming or going.

"Hey, what's up?" I said.

"Hey, Ray. Looks like Dexter's here." I kissed her lovely brown forehead and followed her to the den, where Dexter sat on a sofa watching *Fran*. Olivia tossed her purse on a sky-blue chair and took the shopping bags out of the room, so probably she'd just gotten in. I stood behind the sofa and looked at the TV screen. Dexter was drinking a tall cornered glass of orange juice, the juice thinned to pale yellow, by vodka I guessed. "What's up, Dexter?" I said.

"Home," he said.

There were big stuffed toys positioned on the chairs and on the sofa—a monkey, a bear, a lion, and a big crazy squirrel, sitting up like people. I liked the furniture, large old pieces reupholstered in crosshatched pastel corduroy. Olivia returned in fluffy leopard-print slippers. She said to Dexter, "Why are you watching that?"

I was wondering that, too. It was a big TV, about thirty-five inches.

Dexter shrugged, the ice moving in his glass. "I don't know what I'm supposed to watch," he said, rather helplessly.

"Well," Olivia said, "I guess there's no official statement about what to watch, Dexter."

This was a little funny because sometimes I'd see Olivia on TV reading government announcements or interviewing someone of local importance in her role as a public relations officer for the state. This would be on the government channel, and she'd be wearing a dress in a studio while either she or her guest made official statements. So I chuckled.

I sat on the cushion beside Dexter and next to the stuffed bear. The bear was dark brown and had a white ribbon around its neck. I put the bear between us. I had seen some *Fran* before and I knew it was a stilted show, sketched and loud with canned noise. "Is it good?" I asked. The show had been canceled, I thought. Anyway, it had to be a rerun, in syndication, to be on at that hour. It was news time on most other channels. Dexter usually liked the news. He wrote a column for an alternative local paper, wry and sometimes mordant observations about politics and race.

"It's sort of a cartoon, isn't it?" he said.

Olivia went into the kitchen and began bustling about. I heard pots clanking and glasses clinking. She passed the doorway a couple of times, pretty. I'd always liked the way Olivia looked, sturdy and straight with a happy-to-see-you smile, hair that flounced. She didn't look like a grandmother but she was. Their son, Lee, had baby twins. Everybody had all seemed to settle into it now, but at first there was a problem with the boy being so young and with the girl, also, who was even younger and white—a skinny, quiet girl who had somehow attracted the boy away from overprotective Dexter and Olivia. It was so disappointing because Lee dropped out of college during his freshman year to work for the pregnant girl, who herself dropped out of high school to have the babies. They got married. It was tawdry and sad, too. The girl's parents were non-communicative, the father in jail for fraud of some kind, the mother not too happy about a daughter in love with a black boy. Plus, it seems Lee had first been dating the girl's older sister. But of course, everybody loved the babies, at least Dexter and Olivia did, and the girl had turned out to be a competent mother. Lee had earned admiration for doting on the girl and the babies, working, and taking a class or two at night. Olivia and Dexter babysat a lot, which explained the plush toys.

Absolutely, the whole thing reminded me of myself, how I'd freaked out my folks when I got married out of high school. I was envious of Dexter's boy, who looked like he would get to stay married, whose wife really wanted him—thought he was the sun, the rain, and the stars, as Dexter put it once—but who nevertheless had ruined a possible football career by ditching the scholarship.

"So, we going to this game?" Dexter asked.

"That's what I heard."

A lawyer who often ate lunch at the hotel where I worked had promised me tickets to the Duke-Northwestern game. Luckily it was a night game—lucky for me but not for the lawyer, who had another commitment, as he put it. I didn't have to work. Actually, I was starting a weeklong vacation. In two days, I'd be off to St. John, V.I., courtesy of one of my waiters, Ella, whose husband worked at a travel agency. They got me a plane ticket for next to nothing and a good rate at a villa. It was a group rate, really, with Ella and her sister and their husbands and two of their friends and me. But I'd be essentially traveling alone since I couldn't get a date. My girlfriend, sort of—Alma—backed out when she realized it conflicted with her cousin's wedding in Florida. Then I offered to take *my* cousin Barbara, who I thought might like the treat, but she didn't want her daughter to miss school if she came with us—as if missing a week of sixth grade would damage something—and she didn't want to leave Selena with anybody else, not even her father, who still lived in town. Today I figured if my so-called girlfriend wouldn't go to the Caribbean with me, I'd not waste an effort to invite her to the game. Meanwhile, my cousin Barbara despised football so much she said any woman who claimed to like it was lying.

From work, I'd reached Dexter on his cell phone in the late afternoon. By coincidence, he'd just gotten in from Chicago, where he'd attended a reunion of his Northwestern journalism school class, and was waiting at the airport baggage claim. He didn't really care about the school's football team, and I didn't care about Duke, either. But we had tickets, and we hadn't hung out in a while, especially since the babies were born. He told me, "I'm glad you called. There's a guy with red mutton chops holding a sign that says 'Goddamn Motherfucker.' I was getting ready to hop in his limo."

Now, Dexter raised his glass. "Want a drink?" I said no, later. He drank down a lot of the screwdriver and then got up to take the glass into the kitchen. He drank some more and then put the glass in the sink. He didn't say anything to Olivia, but I couldn't see her so I thought maybe she had gone to another room. Then she came into view holding a large yellow onion, and they moved around each other, in and out of view, as if the other wasn't there. Dexter had on his Tina Turner T-shirt, a picture of Tina Turner in a short black beaded dress doing the shimmy on his chest.

I thought that if Olivia was just getting in, maybe she didn't know why I was there. I said, "Hey, O, I only have two tickets, otherwise I'd have asked you to the game, too." I loved Olivia's name. It was so beautiful I liked to ugly it up as a joke. I liked to make up alternative O names, like Octagon, Ottoman, Oslo. Occasionally, I stumbled upon another beauty, like Oswego. When I couldn't think of one fast I just called her O.

"Why didn't you ask me first, anyway?"

"Really?" I said.

"What game?" she said.

Then Dexter told her, and she put her hand on his waist as he spoke, and he lifted her hand and kissed it. I turned off the TV and waited outside.

He came out in a little while and offered to drive. I was supposed to meet the lawyer at a sports bar near the campus to pick up the tickets, so I directed Dexter there. In the car, I said, "I'm in an expansive frame of mind." I guess I meant I was willing to try to be an extrovert that Saturday night, to get out and have some fun.

After a pause, Dexter said, "That's a peculiar sentence."

"It is?" I asked.

"Yeah. Expansive yet framed. Out there but with limits. As though you want to be free, but not."

"I get it."

"I know that's not what you meant, though."

"I don't know." I thought for a while. Then I asked, "So how was the class reunion?"

"It was okay," Dexter said. "I'm bald, though. That was sort of clear at the reunion."

"That was clear before the reunion."

"Not to them. They hadn't seen me since I started losing hair. I'd tried to tell a few of them over the years, in letters and on the phone and whatnot, making jokes about it, but they weren't used to the sight of me. I kept catching them looking at my head funny, which made me want to put on a hat."

So now I looked at his head. Walnut-colored crown, sparsely gray cropped sides. He'd started getting his hair cut short a few years ago when it was thinning. I guess he could pass for a grandfather now. I was grayer than he was, though a few years younger. I was gray in high school. Premature.

"How are Lee and his family?" I asked. Saying that sounded odd to me, since I wasn't yet used to Lee having a family other than Dexter and Olivia. I was used to Lee being little and playing in the yard with a stick. But Dexter didn't say anything about *that* peculiar sentence. I didn't think Lee was over twenty yet. In fact, I was thinking it was just about a year ago that the twins were born.

"Fine," Dexter said. "Great. You should see them." He had a big grin on his face. "I bought them insurance. The babies are smart."

The sports bar was a rustic open space with wide, scuffed floorboards and wooden tables and chairs and some booths against the wall opposite the bar. TV screens were unavoidable, mounted on the walls, and they showed an old college basketball game on ESPN Sports Classics, women's golf, and a pre-game show for the Duke game. I didn't see the lawyer, so Dexter and I took a middle table and ordered beer. Lighted beer signs spaced along the walls blazed color brighter than that on the TVs, brighter than the three old pinball machines dinging in a corner beside the bar. In the back room, people played pool.

Dexter said, "I come here for lunch sometimes. I think some nights they have a wet pants contest."

We looked around the place for contest announcements. On the table, against the ketchup bottle, was a purple and red plastic card folded and propped up like a tent. It said trivia night was Tuesday. A yellow square of paper under the salt and pepper shakers recruited for a tough man competition in a month; $500 prize money.

"You mean wet T-shirt," I said.

"No. Wet pants. It's their trademark, I think."

"What—contestants drink a lot of beer and get locked out of the bathroom?"

Dexter laughed. "Maybe. Or they sit in a bucket."

I laughed then. "Let's ask the waitress," I said.

The waitress had dark maroon hair and dark blue eyes. She wore frayed wide-legged jeans and a tight pink top with a picture of a baby's pacifier. She slid about in green rubber flip-flops. When she set the cardboard coasters advertising an expensive foreign beer on the table, and then placed our cheap domestic brands on them, I watched her thin arms and hands and then her eyes and long black lashes. She was beautiful. Pink lips. There was a space of creamy skin showing at the waist where the top and jeans separated.

"Anything else, guys?" she asked.

"Nope," Dexter said.

"Nope. Thanks," I said.

When she was gone, Dexter said, "You didn't ask her."

"Why didn't you?"

"You wanted to know." He chuckled.

I looked to the waitress, who went to the end of the bar by the pinball machines. She picked up a burning cigarette from the black plastic ashtray on the bar top and took a puff. It didn't look like she knew how to smoke.

"I couldn't say 'wet butt' to that girl."

"It's wet pants. I think I could say it to her. I think she drinks a lot of milk."

"She certainly has calcium-rich lashes. Her bones look good."

"And her skin," Dexter said.

We drank some beer and watched people come into the room, take seats at tables and at the bar. Pretty soon the place was noisy, people eating and drinking, looking up at the big TV screens, shouting. The lawyer wasn't among them.

"What the lawyer look like," Dexter asked.

"Male, white, blond," I said. "Round. He has a yellow beard."

Everybody in the place was white, or appeared to be, except us and one of the waitresses, an extra cute young brown-skinned woman with straight red-dyed hair and an amber eyebrow stud. Most looked like college students. Most were male. One guy was standing in a corner taking pictures, wearing a many-pocketed khaki vest and his Duke cap backward. Another guy, really short, went around to tables trying to sell flowers, of all things, spooking the women. The TVs all flicked to the same channel now, the football game.

After a while longer, when the place seemed all sound and light, and we were asked if we wanted more beer, it was clear that the lawyer wasn't coming, or that he'd be so late it wouldn't matter. So we ordered a pitcher and some wings. The waitress seemed happy about that order. "Wings are our specialty," she said.

Dexter said, "What about those wet pants?"

She looked alarmed and glanced down at her jeans, touching her thighs and her butt. "Whoa. Thank goodness, not again. Don't tease me, man."

She brought the beer right away, cleared away our empties and set down fresh mugs, all without comment or eye contact.

"Enjoy," she said finally.

"You made her scared," I told Dexter.

"Yeah, right. You can't scare girls today. We're harmless to them. Which is a problem, because they're the only ones I want. Goddamn, what is it about young women, Ray?"

He seemed actually puzzled. I'd forgotten about the earlier screwdriver, and now, after a couple of beers, young women were a bother to him. I said, "They're pretty, Dexter. That's all."

"I still like the women I liked thirty years ago," he said, "when I first got interested. The thing is, women our age, over-forty women, I don't even know how to hold their bodies."

"You been holding a lot of those bodies?"

"I have to hug them sometimes. At church. I try to imagine something more with them, but I can't."

"Olivia see you hugging at church?"

"Olivia. You love Olivia, don't you? I got a skinny woman fetish. That's recently clear to me. Olivia used to be skinny, remember? Skinnier, anyway. I don't like to hold her so much as I used to." He glanced away from me.

I didn't know the best response. I was very fond of Olivia, all right. I thought she was sexy, but not necessarily because of her size and shape. But not despite it either. Still, the woman I was seeing happened to be young and thin. So I guess I wasn't too interested in hugging church women either.

The wings were served by another person, a guy wearing a knit grass-green shirt and with a dull brass bullet in each earlobe. The wings came with giant celery sticks in a boat-shaped white paper bowl, drenched in red sauce, so they were messy to eat. We made a pile of bones anyway.

I felt embarrassed to hear Dexter say what he had said about Olivia. He and I had been friends since high school, when he moved onto our street with his parents. We'd become better friends over the years, because he was no longer quite the older boy, and we had in common local college education and not-bad jobs. Other schoolmates had gotten into other things, like the military or crime, or out-of-town schools and excellent jobs. We liked to talk about sports and politics and point out pretty girls, but the most intimate talk was usually about Lee. That's as truly personal as we got, Dexter not being shy about his love for his son, whether he was angry, frightened, or proud.

Dexter had brought Olivia home from grad school in Evanston, and I coveted her right away. Of course, I never told him that. And I never told him much about my girlfriends, if I had any. Back when I was married we weren't so close. And really, in all the years since my divorce I seldom brought anybody around him unless she was particularly pleasant, pleasant enough for Olivia. And we never discussed anything really personal about him and Olivia other than his stress at gift-giving times, wanting the sure thing to make her happy.

The noise of the bar rose suddenly as somebody scored a touchdown. Folks in Duke gear and a few in Northwestern shirts whooped and groaned. We watched the end zone celebration, and for a little while I imagined my upcoming trip to the islands, and what it might be like to go there with Olivia. I didn't imagine much. It would be a one-bedroom villa; I could sleep on the couch. We could go to the beach and restaurants, and drink the rum and dance. It was an unsatisfactory fantasy, fueled by guilt and desire.

"I'll tell you what bothers me a lot," Dexter said. "Fat women with little breasts."

"Damn, Dexter."

"That doesn't bother you?"

"No," I said, "it doesn't exactly bother me. It's funny, though."

"How about skinny women with fat legs?"

"Come on, Dexter."

"What? You have to admit there's something wrong with that."

Whenever Dexter started getting crude, I tried to steer the conversation away. Thankfully, even Dexter considered some comments over the top. We knew a guy who worked at a shoe store and the things he had to say about the female customers made us cringe, forget blush. He made us laugh, too, at him mostly.

I pointed to the TV screen, where a Duke player was running long down the sideline. More shouts from the bar patrons. Then the teams traded interceptions. I looked around for the lawyer again, just in case. Finally I saw him. He was sitting at a small table against the wall on the other side of the room, several tables ahead of us. He seemed to be scraping his tongue with a long white tool. I didn't tell Dexter because I didn't want to talk to the lawyer now, anyway. Besides, it was hard to believe he hadn't seen us whenever he came in, sitting in the middle of the room as we were. Really, the guy liked to talk too much and assumed a familiarity we didn't actually have. He liked to tell me about his black clients—young car thieves and drug offenders, mostly. He liked to mimic their speech. Once I asked him if he ever had any white clients. He said he did. I asked, "Why don't you ever mimic them?" He laughed and said, "I'm doing that right now."

I glanced over at him again. He was scraping his tongue, hunched over the table, and writing something on a yellow legal pad.

Dexter said, "That could be Lee out there trying to pick off those passes."

"Lee didn't go to Duke, or Northwestern," I said, looking up at the screen. I didn't mean to sound cutting. Lee had dropped out of decent school, A&T. But it was unlikely that he would have played on TV in college.

"Hell, I know that," Dexter said. "Don't be so literal. He's such a stupid kid, to be so gifted."

I remembered then the day a few years back when Dexter came over to my house cursing and laughing about Lee's alleged stupidity. He had with him a video he'd found in Lee's room, an unlabeled red cassette that Dexter was afraid to watch, especially at home. He suspected it was porn because he'd found it under Lee's mattress while Lee was at school, when they had bought him a new bed. Yet Lee knew they'd be switching out the bed that day and he hadn't bothered to tidy up. Could the boy be that mindless, Dexter wondered? So Dexter hid the tape from Olivia and brought it to me for viewing.

It was called *Cake Eaters* and featured four white couples lounging in an elegant living room after a birthday party, the large white cake partially eaten in the center of the coffee table, and party hats and streamers on the table and floor. A black waiter in a bowtie comes in with a tray of champagne, and then when each person takes a turn describing a fantasy of the perfect birthday, the scene shifts to an enactment of the fantasy, some sexual tableau, including a dominatrix controlling two men. And then two women and a man in a waterfall. Two women in a department store changing room. A dentist and his nurse. A guy in football shoulder pads and a cheerleader. The finale showed the naked party guests smearing cake on each other. The most memorable scene was a woman's jungle fantasy, a blonde asleep on a canopied bed draped with mosquito netting in a rainforest. A naked black man, the waiter with paint marking his face, shows up and rubs against her through the netting. She puts various parts of herself against him, but there's always the net barrier, and he finally convulses and then slinks back into the jungle. We watched all of it, sitting on opposite ends of my couch, drinking Cokes and eating popcorn I made when we stopped the tape once. When we were done, Dexter stashed the tape at my house until Lee finally asked for it, said he had to give it back to the kid he'd borrowed it from.

Since then, Dexter and I joked about that mosquito net scene. We called it "romancing the veil," "the veil of love." It became a catch-all reference anytime we perceived some obstacle to somebody's desire. Later, when Lee revealed that his high school girl was pregnant, we said he had gone beyond the veil. Still, veils are everywhere. That I would have to go on vacation alone, the first real vacation I'd had ever, a vacation practically given to me—well, that was a veil. That Olivia had met and married Dexter, lovely Olivia who was just my type, perfectly suited to me, that was a veil. That my young wife had left me after two years while I had imagined a happy old-age death with her, that was a veil. I looked at the TV and couldn't focus on who had the ball. The beer was making me morose.

I got up to go to the bathroom, beyond the pool tables. That's where I saw the Wet Pants Contest signs, posted on the walls outside the "Gods" and "Goddettes" doors, next to a framed basketball jersey. Field hockey sticks were mounted crisscrossed on the wall.

Women only for the contest, it seemed; $500 to the winner of that one, too. The signs still did not explain how the pants got wet. I wondered were they wet pants or wet underpants that people competed with. On my way back, I was thinking that a dry underpants contest would be just as good, when I saw our waitress delivering another pitcher of beer to our table.

I knew, finally, that Dexter didn't need more to drink. In high school and college, we'd survived three wrecks and a street fight caused by his drinking, and each time I'd started out trusting him to know what he was doing. But in twenty years I'd rarely seen him drink too much, not since Lee was born. Now I considered that it wasn't Dexter's drinking that was ever so much the problem as it was my trusting him. So, fine, we could get a cab. We could have another pitcher.

I sat down and he said, "You want to meet some friendlier women?"

"Sure," I said. I remembered quickly that I was on vacation, that I was in an expansive frame of mind, and that I didn't really have much of a girlfriend if she wouldn't go to an all-expense-paid Caribbean party with me. I was feeling buzzed with beer, sad and mad. I said, "Hell yeah," although it didn't sound like me saying it.

Then Dexter told me that I had to go to Chicago, that he had found a house there where the women were young and pretty and thin. All races. And they treated you like they loved you. He said you go in a living room with a cream-colored carpet, and this smiling girl comes out and talks to you, gives you a drink, massages your shoulders, kisses your ear, takes you into a nice bedroom with rose-colored sheets and makes love to you.

I was shocked that Dexter had gone to a whorehouse in Chicago. I had thought maybe he knew somebody from his paper that I could meet. Somewhere nearby.

"She acts like she wants nothing more than to please you, and like you please her. She clings to you when it's time for you to leave," Dexter said.

"What's her name?" I asked.

"Hell, Ray, you won't believe it. This girl said her name was Olive."

"Jesus."

"Yeah. That was a problem for about five minutes. After that, I figured it was fine, fitting. She had pretty olive skin. I just wish she *were* Olivia. I wish Olivia were she. I wish I could really be loved like that."

I poured beer in each glass. I said, "But you are loved, man. Better." Neither of us sounded quite familiar now.

"Just not like that," he said.

Who *was*, I wondered? It wasn't even love, compared to what Dexter did have. Even I knew that—I, as the old song says, who have nothing. I drank some beer and considered for a minute why I had nothing. What did I have? A small business, a few friends, a cousin and a niece, a house, a kind of girlfriend, money in my pocket and a little bit in the bank, an ability to want intensely and then to stop. Not bad. I'd learned about the latter when my wife divorced me. The problem was that I could stop and then start again, too.

The redheaded brown-skinned waitress came through with a big tray of food and bottles, and I had to scoot my chair up for her to get by. She had good form with the tray, a languid, confident quality. She left a delicate flower scent, totally unexpected for a girl in desert camouflage. I watched her with her arms raised, walking loose-hipped in the low-slung pants, watched her bend to dispense the bottles and plates. I went from imagining her working for me to imagining her long arms around me. It was as dumb a desire as any, to want something I couldn't have, given the likelihood that she wouldn't want an old guy like me. I wondered why I wanted what was so difficult to have. I wondered if I preferred romancing the veil

"Romancing the veil," I said.

"Not me," said Dexter. He laughed. "Not in Chicago anyway."

I said, "Yeah, that's sort of hard to know what to do with."

"Believe me," he winked, "you'd know what to do with it."

"I'm talking about your wife," I said. "And your old self."

"My old self? Ray, I have been this old for fifteen years. For the last five Olivia has been sick of me and I have been sick of that. We have been hanging around for Lee, basically. Now that he's all fucked, and we're baby-addled grandparents, I'm just living with the postponement of heartbreak. And Chicago hasn't changed any of that. Understand that Olivia, if she knew, would merely have more reason not to want me."

He slouched down in his chair and turned his gaze back to the TV. A commercial was on. "Are you guys breaking up? Are you talking divorce or something?" I asked.

"Probably. Maybe." He looked at me quickly, then the TV again.

I felt a sudden emptiness, a struggle to breathe. People were up and moving about, bumping into me. Our table seemed the one in the way of all traffic. Out of the shifting appeared the lawyer, who scraped back a chair and sat down. He plopped his legal pad on the table beside the pitcher of beer.

"So," he said. "Been waiting long?" He laughed a long time, so that I started to think the whole thing was a practical joke involving the game tickets and Dexter's confessions. "Sorry. I know I was supposed to be here, but guess what. I got busy. I lost the tickets. My ex came over with some nonsense you don't want to know about." He stopped. He threw up his hands and said, "Actually, my father-in-law died. That's why I offered you the tickets in the first place, but I left them at my ex-wife's house and I don't want to go back there for them." He looked at Dexter and at me. "Your friend?" he asked.

"Yes," I said. "Dexter, this is James Jabowski, the guy we were supposed to meet."

"Jab," he said. He thrust out his hand to shake. "My apologies. Things happen. The game's not that good anyway, I'll bet."

"It's tied," Dexter said.

"The worst kind," the lawyer said.

"James," I said. "Where have you really been?"

"Jab," he said.

"Since when are you Jab? Didn't you see us when you came in, what, thirty minutes ago?"

"Today is my birthday. I'm thirty-fizzle, my nizzle, and I've decided that I'm Jab for the rest of my dizzles."

"The rest of your dinners?" Dexter asked. He sat up and squinted at James, but slid back into his slouch, his hands cupped around his beer glass.

"Why are you saying *nizzle*, James? Are you still among the sane?"

"Has he ever been?" Dexter asked.

"I don't know," I said. James was always a bit nutty, someone who liked to laugh and kid about everything and himself. I'd never seen him away from the hotel, where he came to eat, often alone, usually reading or writing something. He always wore a suit and tie, and his professional garb tended to mitigate his jokes. Now he wore a suit but no tie and he was stranger than ever. The yellow hair hanging over his forehead was twisted into four ratty dreadlock-like strands. He had gray circles under his eyes, which were bloodshot and electric blue behind rimless glasses. Maybe he was drunk.

"*Schnizzle*, then," he said. "Ray, you're not married, right?"

"Right."

"What about you, bud?"

"Wrong," Dexter said.

"It's Dexter," I said. "Or Dex."

Dexter smiled.

"Today's my birthday," James said again, and paused expectantly. But we were waiting for him to explain why he had repeated it. Finally we said happy birthday. James said, "My father-in-law died on my birthday. He was my enemy in life, and now in death he hassles me. I was going to the game in celebration of my birthday, but I thought, no, I'll spend it with my mother. I was gonna surprise *her* on my birthday. But when I got there my ex-wife was already sitting down talking to her, and that surprised *me*. They gave me a going-over, saying to me, 'Look at yourself,' which was no celebration at all. Mama asked me to take her to my father-in-law's house, to visit the family there. All right, I do, and all the while my ex keeps telling me I owe her money. Hell, she makes more than me, and half the debt's in her name. I emptied my pockets. I had $43.27, some saltwater taffy, and the tickets. I left everything there on the kitchen table next to pies and potato salad people had brought over. I kept my wallet, though." He slid over his legal pad. "I been jotting down a few notes that come to me since that visit, a draft of my midlife thoughts. What do you think?"

The page was written on with a fat-tipped black pen, the letters printed and square. The heading read: *The 4 Freedoms*. But it had been amended from three freedoms. There were actually seven items on the list.

1. *Freedom from Sameness (everybody can't be the same)*
2. *Freedom of Religion (there's a lot of them)*
3. *Freedom from Religion (I am free from religion)*
4. *Freedom from Tyranny*
5. *Never get a wife who thinks she's better than you*
6. *Never, never have anything to do with her family*
7. *Do not allow women to rearrange your apartment*

"What is this, Jab?" Dexter asked.

"It's what I've learned reinforced by today's lectures and indictments against me for not being 'right.'" He made finger quotes by his ears. "My mama and my wife, my *ex*-wife I wish she would understand, and without rights to fuck with me anymore, are in a loose cahoots. I don't know why. My mama still has rights, can't help that, but them together need an injunction in the form of what I've produced on this paper."

"What about numbers 5 through 7?" I asked.

"It's not parallel, I know that. It's just a draft."

Dexter said, "I take it you lost the desire to hug your wife."

"And my mama, too, now," James said.

"That's too bad," I said. "I'm sorry."

"Yeah, it has put me in a bind. Especially on my birthday. They told me my *breath* stinks. They told me I'm bound for hell. But the real sonofabitch is my father-in-law who died today. He *always* makes me feel like shit."

"My marriage is dissolving," Dexter said.

James and I stared at him. He was down in the mouth. Then James laughed.

He said, "Man, marriages don't dissolve. I wish to hell they did."

Our maroon-haired waitress came back, smiling. A young Audrey Hepburn, I decided. Dexter and I refused more beer and gave her money. During that transaction, James gaped at her, but then went back to work on his list.

I said, "James, we're leaving. Thanks for offering the tickets. It got us out of the house, at least, if not to the game."

"You're welcome," he said. "Y'all think that shorty's tight, right?" He nodded toward our waitress, who was tending another table. "You think she beautiful. Well, she just make herself *look* beautiful. Those silky bangs, smoky eyes, all *made* to be cute like that. Look critically, playboys. It ain't all *all*."

He wrote down another freedom:

8. *Freedom from fakes*

We left him at our table, polishing his list, finishing our beer. Outside was windy. Rows of cars gleamed under the yellowish parking lot lamps. For a moment I was disoriented. I forgot who drove, and was a little stunned to be away from the inside noise and into the warm, gray, illuminated night.

"Ah, hell," Dexter said. He pointed across a row of cars to his silver station wagon, the chrome luggage rack gleaming. A few guys were leaning against the car as if it belonged to them.

When we got there, Dexter said, "Excuse us, fellows," and they slowly moved aside, barely giving us room to get in and pull out of the space. There were three of them, white guys in hip-hop outfits— basketball jerseys, big jackets, big pants, jewelry. As Dexter put it in drive and rolled forward, we heard a knock on the back panel of the car. It wasn't loud, more like a hard pat you'd give a horse's rump, to make it go or to praise it, *a good old horse*. But Dexter stopped the car and got out. I got out, too, wishing Dexter hadn't, and walked around to check for damage. There wasn't any that I could see.

These were big boys, tall and heavy, their bulky coats open over jerseys and big T-shirts. Their big clean workboots were unlaced. We were tinted red by the wagon's taillights. Dexter said, "Guys, was that necessary?"

"What?" they said, almost together.

"You know, if you had dented my car, you could have been arrested for vandalism."

One, in a purple and gold Lakers jersey and a light, loosely knit skullcap, laughed, turning to the others. "Fuck you, man. Nobody touched your punk-ass car."

"Hey, asshole," I said, but couldn't form a finish, my anger was so sudden. It confused me. I felt my face burning and my heart galloping. I couldn't understand these white boys, acting black, giving us a hard time. First James, and now these jerks. Or maybe it wasn't about race, just younger guys flexing power. Whatever, it caused me to suck in an extremely deep breath and blow it out. It was like Popeye getting steamed before a fight, the fiery ash erupting from his corncob pipe, a ship on his bicep shooting out smoke. I was shaking.

Yet Dexter was calm. He said, "Fellows, all I'm trying to say is that you should be more careful, think before you do stupid stuff. You don't need to ruin your lives." His speech was a little slurred. "Especially harassing people you don't even know."

The boys stared at us, flexing their many-ringed fingers, nodding threateningly.

"Shit," one of them said, a sparkly K hanging from a thick silver chain around his neck. It looked encrusted with rubies in the red taillights of Dexter's car.

"Shit," another one said, almost a whisper. He kept touching his mustache, a carefully trimmed little line that streaked down to his preened goatee.

"All right," Dexter said. "We're out."

As we got back into the station wagon, the first one said, "I'll ruin *your* life, man. My mother's the fucking D.A.!"

I looked back at him. He was smacking his heart with his fist, his chin raised.

Behind the wheel, Dexter said, "Jesus. Kids."

"His mama's the D.A.?" I asked.

"That's what he said. Poor woman."

"Man, didn't you want to kick him in the nuts?"

"Hell, we'd have lost some teeth, Ray. Our bones would be broken. Besides, we're grownups."

"Yeah, you're right about all that, I guess."

Dexter drove well. We got to his house and I couldn't find my keys. They weren't in my pockets, they weren't in my ignition, and they weren't behind the cushions in Dexter's den. So I took Dexter's car to get home, thinking of the spare house key taped under the mailbox on my porch. But on the way I came upon a roadblock. When I saw the cop lights ahead, I pulled into somebody's driveway, cut my lights, waited a few minutes, and then turned around. I suspected I'd drunk enough to be in trouble. One of the cop cars caught up to me pretty quickly. Things got worse when I couldn't find Dexter's registration and insurance cards in the glove box or over the visor, the only places I knew to look.

"It's not my car," I told him.

He suspected I'd stolen it. He thought I was drunk when I couldn't say the ABCs backward. I stumbled when I couldn't remember where Q was, the order of M and N. I thought I was going to jail. Look, I thought, where an expansive frame of mind had gotten me.

The policeman put me in the backseat of the patrol car. I sat behind his partner who occupied the passenger seat. They didn't have a breathalyzer kit in the car. They got on the radio and called for one. Meanwhile, as they ran a computer search of my driver's license, I explained again whose car I'd been driving, why I was in it, where Dexter lived, where my car was. I was polite, nervous, trying to seem innocent and perfectly reasonable. I told them I'd just started my vacation, the first in forever. I told them about my job—my business—operating the waitstaff at the hotel. I thought but did not say, *I'm no criminal, occifer; I'm a respectable bidnessman.*

"That's a lot of information," the first one said. "Why don't you know your alphabet?"

The second one snickered.

I listened to them talk about their kids' fundraising efforts for their elementary school's Harvest Festival. They talked about the

Duke game, too, and I tried to figure out who had won. I wanted to join their conversation, to say I'd watched some of the game. But I was all but ignored. They didn't care about me. My pleas and politeness were nothing to them. They were merely working, like fishermen with tonight's catch gasping in the backseat. There were no controls for the windows and no handles for the doors back there. I listened to them through the opened slot in the Plexiglas barrier.

I got mad again. I wanted to curse out the cops. Some vacation. I thought about my girlfriend, who never offered me the least bit of emotional comfort. And I thought, what's the difference, really, between a vacation alone in the Caribbean and one alone in jail? I'd be lonesome and hangdog either way, just glancing at different scenery through the barred or palmed veil. Outside the hazy back window was a half moon. The car's bright blue lights swept rhythmically against the pine trees at the side of the road.

Then I thought about Dexter at home with Olivia, asleep beside her pleasant body.

Suddenly I felt sad for their sadness, that they were no longer in love, that even what looked good finally wasn't. The temperature was dropping. The vinyl upholstery felt cool to my fingers. I put my hands in my lap. I took deep breaths to steady myself against the anger, the sadness, the fear of being jailed for DUI. Alma, my cousin Barbara, people at work, everybody who knew me would take a different view now. My business could suffer. I knew, though, that if I went to jail tonight I'd be out in a day. There'd be court and attorney fees. I guessed I could call James. I shuddered to think of that.

I'd been in the car a long time. The cops had checked the state's computers about Dexter's plates. I felt fine, except still scared. I wondered if I could pass a breathalyzer test now. I doubted I could pass a lie detector test. The driver turned back to me and asked again why I was driving that car. I told again about losing my keys. I explained again who Dexter was, *the local columnist*, where exactly he lived, *not far from here, behind the mall.* "You could call him," I said. The second cop thought he had read Dexter's columns. He told me to say the ABCs again, and I did better. They told me I seemed sober enough, that I was to drive Dexter's car straight back to where it belonged, and that the reason they'd stopped me was because the station wagon had a taillight out.

A taillight. They were both on at the sports bar parking lot during the confrontation with those irritating boys. I didn't tell the policemen about that. I asked if I could just drive home. I was almost there. "No," they said.

So I drove back to Dexter's. I thought I'd just sleep on the couch, with the bear. I knocked, rang the bell, pounded, but nobody answered. Deter was probably passed out, but Olivia should have heard. Maybe she slept with earplugs. Maybe they both did. Maybe she was passed out, too.

I looked back at the station wagon ticking in the driveway, bordered by the low white landscape lights and blooming yellow chrysanthemums. I could sleep in there, pull down the seat. Shiver through the slumbering morning. Then I looked in on Olivia's car in the garage. I raised the door, found her key on Dexter's key ring, and drove her Subaru to my house. I avoided the roadblock, didn't see another cop.

The next morning I called and said I had Olivia's car. I tried to explain, but they were slow to process it, busy on another phone call, and getting breakfast and getting dressed for church. Olivia told me to come for dinner and I could clear it up then. Meanwhile, they'd drive the station wagon.

I pulled up about two. Dexter opened the door. He still had on his suit pants and necktie, his shirt cuffs unbuttoned and turned. I got a whiff of his cologne, and he made me think of my father, who loved Sundays, used to wake up singing hymns.

"How're they hugging?" I asked.

"Thickly. What happened to you last night?" He led me through the foyer into the den.

"I got detained, that's what. Cops. Threat and intimidation. Pinned me for a drunk and a thief."

"No shit? But what are you doing with Olivia's car?"

Dexter's granddaughters sat on the beige rug, pale little girls playing with toy horses. They had on red plaid dresses and had cherry barrettes in their braided light hair. They were tiny. That was disconcerting because I thought they were at least a year old, but they looked about eight or nine months.

"Hey, little girls," I said.

One of them stood up and walked to Dexter, who picked her up. The other stared up at me with wide-open eyes, looking to see what would happen next, if I would do something funny or scary, maybe. The one in Dexter's arms pointed at the keys in my hand. "That?" she asked.

"That's Papa's keys," Dexter answered. He took them from me and jangled them for the baby. The other one got up and walked into the kitchen. She came back holding Olivia's hand. I couldn't believe they could walk and talk, small as they were. They were like midget babies, or genius babies.

Olivia said, "Dexter, can't you keep them in here?" He pointed to me, then set his baby down with the other one. Olivia said, "Hey, Ray."

"Ola," I said. She laughed.

Dexter grabbed a colorful advertisement from the Sunday paper on the coffee table, balled it up, and tossed it on the floor between the girls. They fell upon it giggling.

"Like kittens," he said, and tossed another one. "They're having a wet pants contest right now," he said.

I asked, "Is Lee here?" I hadn't seen Lee in a long time. I'd met his wife once.

"They went to get DVDs. You seen the paper?" he asked.

"I called you and I went back to sleep."

He thrust the front page at me. In the center, above the fold, was a color photo of us at the sports bar gazing off at a TV, me with a chicken wing paused at my lips.

"Good gracious," I said. I laughed. I'd never had my picture in the paper before.

The caption read, *Fans Cheer Duke to Victory.*

"It's a chicken commercial." Dexter chuckled.

"The press makes the place look integrated."

"You can't believe what you see in the paper."

"That's a bona fide fact."

"Here's something else you can't believe." He retrieved another section of the paper, the obituaries. I recognized a picture of James Jabowski, without the dreadlocked bangs, posed and serious in his eyeglasses and tie. But the obituary was for his father-in-law.

"Man, he must be freaking out over this," I said. "How could that happen? You think his wife did this? Is she as evil as James thinks she is?"

"She couldn't be. This is her father's obit, after all. Probably the mortuary's screw-up. Cosmic wrongness."

I sat beside Dexter and put the paper back on the table. Things were wrong, all right. This house, for instance, felt nothing but harmonious. Things with Dexter and Olivia seemed fine, despite what Dexter had said last night. From the windows, white sunlight fell where the girls played on the floor.

I thought of James's manifesto. I wondered what he would add to it after he saw the obituary. As for my embarrassing picture in the paper, there was nothing I could do about that. At least, I assumed, there was no back-page mention of my run-in with the cops. So I looked at the baby girls. They were making the horses prance on the balled-up flyers from the paper. A cartoon was on TV, low-volume loopy clarinet music with leaping garden tools.

The house smelled great, like something succulent roasting in the oven, something sweet just baked, like spicy tea brewing. I wished my girlfriend, Alma, were here. I thought about asking Olivia if I could bring her to dinner. She'd say yes, of course. But I just sat there, listening to the sophisticated baby talk, and I thought about tomorrow. I tried to conjure the Caribbean, the turquoise sea, the white sand, the pink hibiscus and warm sun. I'd be on vacation, somewhere completely different, as if that's where I wanted to be.

The Burrison Prize

THE BURRISON LITERARY PRIZE LUNCHEON WAS OF INTEREST TO
Ray for three reasons: he had begun a creative writing class on Tuesday nights and his teacher was a candidate for the prize; his friend
Dexter had surprised everyone by writing and publishing a novel that
was also nominated this year; and it was a showcase for his serving
business, Triangle Ray, that contracted to the hotel. Ray was managing the staff that would serve the hundred guests.

The cocktail reception was held in the lobby outside the doors of
the hotel's Evergreen Room. Four of his bartenders took care of two
bars at opposite ends of the room. Long tables against the middle wall
held copies of the twelve nominated books, all vying to be named the
year's best book of fiction by a North Carolina writer, as stipulated by
the Burrison Literary Prize Committee and the writers they had hired
to judge. Dressed-up people milled about, most sipping gin and tonics
with lime, or chilled white wine, the pale gold color complementing
the light spring hues of the women's silk and linen clothes. A few men
wore blue or brown seersucker suits, solid knit ties or bright striped
silks. Others wore blazers or Madras plaid jackets with ties. All were
book club members and patrons of the arts taking the opportunity to
hobnob with the artists—people who had time on a Thursday between
eleven and two to get buzzed, have a meal, and listen to literary talk.

Ray looked around for Dexter. His would be one the few dark faces among the guests, although a lot of people were already ostentatiously tanned for mid-April. Betty Daye, the Burrison Prize committee president, was one such person. She looked luxurious in a long, flowing dress of tiered shades of turquoise. She had her long frosted hair piled loosely atop her head, and moved quickly from task to task with bracelets of silver and large chunks of turquoise snicking along her gesturing wrists. A big blue-green spear of the stone stretched along the middle finger of her right hand, while a bright diamond sparked on her left. A few minutes ago, she had confirmed with Ray the number of vegetarian plates and asked for a table on which to set the large, etched crystal bowl that would be given to the winner. Even her eyes were turquoise, with bursts of yellow surrounding the pupils. She was a beautiful old woman, the kind that fascinated Ray for her ability to overwhelm a person with graciousness while never allowing him to rally an equal response. Betty Daye was like a stage actress, with exaggerated manners that Ray would have felt like a fool trying to match. But such was the life of a servant in the South, Ray had observed. He could suppress his aversion and play the soft-spoken roles of minion and audience to the ruling exhibitionists.

While instructing Yusuf, a young waiter from UNC, to set up a table on the platform behind the lectern and to put a white cloth on it, Ray spotted his writing teacher, Abby Bishop, talking with a man who was almost as short as she was, and whose yellowish white hair was slicked back with deep comb tracks. Abby was drinking wine. A gold, emerald-eyed, spread-winged bug perched on a shoulder of her hot pink jacket. This was funny, because in class she was against ornamentation and disdained self-consciousness. Ray was afraid of her, for unlike Betty Daye, who made him feel inferior, Abby Bishop made him feel dumb. She gave back Ray's stories with adjectives, adverbs, and whole passages crossed out, and with marginal notes like

"Muddy," "Huh?" and "What's at stake?" When she held forth about psychic distance, Ray wasn't sure what she meant. But he went over to wish her good luck.

"Hey, Teach," he said. "I hope you win."

"Hello there, Fielding. You look sharp."

He wore the white waistcoat with the white shirt, black bowtie, black pants and shoes. "Thanks," he said. "You, too." He eyed the bug on her shoulder, a dragonfly, its four wings made of gold mesh, a tiny diamond at the tip of its tail. "That's quite a specimen."

"Meet my husband," she said. "He gave it to me. Putty, this is Ray Fielding, the waiter-slash-writer."

Putty nodded, shook hands. "I've heard about you folks. Abby needs to get over to the table and sign some books. Sounds like a funky class."

"Funky, funky," Ray said, snapping his fingers, bouncing a little. He felt nervous. It was always a little awkward running into people he knew from other areas of his life at work, even though he'd known Abby would be here today. But he'd never ever pretended to be casual in her presence, and this was the place he should be most professional, the least casual. Or was it? This was his domain. Except his domain was always dominated by those he served.

"I teach geology," Putty said, "so there's hardly any getting to know my students." His speech was slurred by a mouth that could only half smile. A stroke mouth, probably.

"It's a class of nuts, isn't it, Fielding?" Abby said. "Y'all excuse me to do my duty." She gave Putty her wineglass, mostly full, and scuttled off to the book table.

"Geology, huh?" Ray said.

"Yeah."

"Not entomology? The fancy bug and all."

"I should have given her a nice piece of gypsum?"

"It's a stunning insect. You made the better choice."

"Abby tells me you wrote a good story. She says you're one of her best."

"No kidding?" Ray looked at her back as she bent over the autograph table. She was a square-shaped woman, built like a box. "That's really sweet of her to say."

Putty slurped a laughed. "No, no. Abby is not sweet. If she said it, she meant it."

"Well, I'll tell you, that's more than flattering. It's flabbergasting."

"I'll tell her you said so."

"Oh, no. Please don't. But that's good news. I needed that."

"Who doesn't like praise?"

"I broke up with my girlfriend last night."

"So you did need it. It's not better than a girlfriend, though."

"I guess."

"Maybe you'll meet someone here. Life is full of the species, you know. Just look."

"Thanks, but I'm done for a while. Took forever to get out of that confusion."

"Yeah, it doesn't make sense, does it?"

"I wonder what Abby liked," Ray said, needing more.

"The three pigs, I think."

"Oh, cool. The fairy tale riff she asked us to do. Mine was about a home invasion. Did she tell you about the woman who reworked Snow White? Ms. White's being pimped by the dwarves? After the prince saves her, she plans to introduce him to Jesus, when they would live happily ever after."

"The real Jesus?"

"That's what I wondered. Mixing up the fairy tales. Maybe just his ideas."

"Genre blending," Putty said.

Ray saw Dexter enter the room. The cocktail crowd had thinned some as people wandered into the dining room to stake claims to tables. He could see his waiters pouring coffee for some of the guests. The water glasses had been filled, ice already disappearing.

"Guess what," he said to Putty. "I'm working."

"See ya," Putty said. He looked at the wineglasses he held, one in each hand. "There's supposed to be a drunk writer or two at these things. I might give 'em some competition today."

Maybe that's what it took to be married to Abby Bishop, Ray thought. Drinks. Although sober, he too sort of loved her right then. He made it over to Dexter, who was talking to two women by the Evergreen Room entrance. They were beautiful women, young, neither one Dexter's wife, who, Ray knew, wouldn't make it. She had to work, she said, when Ray called their house last night.

"This is Selma and this is Milla," Dexter said, introducing them. "My buddy, Ray," he said to the women.

"Nice outfit," Selma said. She had a massive spray of curly, sand-colored hair.

Ray said, "I work here." He brushed the lapels of the waistcoat. "Are you up for the prize, too?" He wouldn't have been surprised if she were. He knew to expect to be astonished by the young. Teenagers drove to the hotel in Aston Martins, Ferraris, and Bentleys, living lives full of confidence. With the band that entertained in the hotel lounge on weekends, a fourteen-year-old played guitar like Charlie Christian. Some of his college waiters seemed to know more about the wide world than he, at forty-two, did. These women looked to be in their twenties.

"We work with Dexter at the paper," Selma replied. "He paid our way. And we like him."

"Groupies," Dexter said.

"Yeah," said Selma.

The other woman, Milla, hadn't said anything, had barely looked at Ray, he noticed. She was the more alluring. She gazed out at the guests with startling dark blue eyes. She had pale skin and a long nose, her straight dark hair in a low ponytail. "You're not from the United States, are you, Milla?" Ray asked.

"I'm from Europe," she said, turning to him, smiling, crossing one neat foot over the other and clasping her hands at her narrow waist. She wore a white blouse and a gray slender skirt. Her shoes were gray heels. "I was born in Bosnia, but I grew up in Germany." Not much of an accent. Her voice seemed to come from deeper inside her than most people's.

"Intern," said Dexter. "Exchange student. Northwestern. My alma mater."

"Of course," Ray said. "I hope you like our modest America." Dexter hadn't mentioned he'd bring company. Ray pointed Dexter toward the book table. "You're supposed to sit over there and sign for whoever buys your novel."

There were nametags for the authors in front of folding chairs at the table. Abby Bishop sat at hers, now, but few of the others were claimed. Over the course of the reception, writers came and went from the table. At the moment, a tall man in a white Panama hat and a cinched black terrycloth bathrobe had the most attention. Under the robe showed a shirt and tie.

"Who's that?" Milla asked.

"The most assured," Dexter said. "Bobby Router, author of *Socks*. It's about a half-breed, bisexual schizophrenic."

"Autobiographical, I'll bet. He looks like a lot of things," Selma said.

"Not much time before lunch is served," Ray said. "You want to sit there for ten minutes? After that, you have to go in there and get the prize."

"Yeah, right. My little book about a child snail collector doesn't stand a chance against conepone tomes about Great-Grandma's sewing basket or magic mud pie."

"That's the one I want to read," Selma said. "I love magic food fiction."

"What's cornpone?" Milla asked.

"*Cone*pone," Dexter said. "A genre of literature."

"Ever had mud pie?" Selma asked.

"No, not ever," Milla said.

"It's chocolate."

"I like chocolate."

"I have to check on some stuff," Ray said. "Good luck, man," he told Dexter.

"Serve like the wind," Selma said.

The waiters knew their serving zones. The kitchen had rolled the warming carts containing the covered lunches to the side hallway. From the hall, three sets of double doors led into the Evergreen Room, and all the staff had to do was load up two, three, or four plates, depending on their skill, and place them in front of the guests. Two or three would work a table to get the food out fast, then separate for the rest of the meal to replenish drinks, one person to cover three tables of eight. For dessert, they'd regroup for fast clearing and serving. Ray would help out if he was needed, but mostly to show the others that he was a part of the team.

Authors' nametags were on the dining tables, too. Each table would seat at least one of the nominated writers, a souvenir memory for the non-writers who came for the $75 lunch. The guest speaker was seated at the front of the room near the raised podium, behind which was now a white cloth-covered table and the large crystal bowl. Ray strolled among the round banquet tables, checking again that everything looked right, and noting where Abby Bishop and Dexter would sit.

Soon, Dexter and his coworkers took their seats near the middle doors on the side of the room. White-haired women shared that table. Ray tried to take note of who the other nominees were, so few had manned the autograph table. He had recognized some famous names on the place tags. He figured the few men with beards, the black woman with cowry shells in her hair, and the heavy blond guy in the wrinkled blue silk shirt were among the honored, as were a couple of thin white women with unstyled hair wearing long lank skirts and flat shoes. If seating were any indication of rank, then Abby ranked high, her table with Putty directly behind that of Betty Daye and the guest speaker at the front.

The speaker's book was co-written with a more famous writer—a young white woman from the speaker's home state of Georgia. It had been widely praised. Ray had not read it, but it was supposed to be an unflinching portrait of poverty and illiteracy in the rural South. It chronicled the guest speaker's life of violence and deprivation, a life of cunning, compassion, and indomitable spirit. These were words in the brief biography printed on the luncheon's program. According to reviews, the man, a black man, Donny "Buck" Tate, had fathered eighteen children with various women, and had managed through many hardships—including prison and brain surgery—to find redemption through his late effort to claim and bring together his extended family. He and the co-writer, Tina Cockburn (pronounced Cokeburn), had appeared together on talk shows. Tina Cockburn wasn't here today. Donny "Buck" Tate had a large brown bald spot in the middle of his bushy, suspiciously black hair. Ray couldn't tell how old he was, but late sixties at least. He wore a brown suit with a yellow shirt. He sat quietly at his table accompanied by Betty Daye and other Burrison Prize dignitaries, sipping iced tea.

While the plates were being served, Betty Daye stood at the lectern before the crystal bowl and explained the occasion. She told anecdotes about Dennis Burrison, the liberal newsman who, in the sixties, championed civil rights and mentored, she said, directly or indirectly, every major journalist in the South. She told of when she herself worked in his newsroom, how he ruthlessly edited her work, sent her on assignments, and drank and flirted with her. "Dennis Burrison was a lover. A lover of people, of truth, and of language," she said. "But he would have been as astounded as proud that the prize for literature given in his name has held such prestige for now twenty-two years. The writers who have received it are among the best in the nation, let alone the South, and of course they represent the cream of our great state of North Carolina. This year's nominees are no less wonderful. They are sitting at your tables! Say hello to them!" People laughed, applauded, and nodded at their own personal authors. The authors nodded back, and Ray saw that he was right about some of his guesses.

As Betty Daye wrapped up her speech, instructing the diners to "Eat! Eat!" Ray slipped out to the lobby. Lunch and dessert would take about twenty or thirty minutes. Then Tate would speak. Then the judges would announce the winner. Everything should be completed in about an hour, an hour and a half. The bars would remain open. The bartenders, ever efficient, had already replenished ice, sliced limes, cherries, stirrers, and napkins. One was reading *Entertainment Weekly*, another was hunched over a novel she must have borrowed from the book table. The room was empty of guests, and familiar sounds of cutlery on plates and the murmuring crowd issued mutedly through the closed Evergreen Room doors.

In the side hall, Ray checked the warming carts for leftover lunches. He lifted the silver top off one plate. A small quarter of broiled chicken, asparagus, and new potatoes. The vegetarian cart was empty, except for a round red-skinned potato that had fallen onto the speckled blue carpet. He picked it up. It was warm and moist, oily.

His girlfriend, ex-girlfriend, now off-again-forever thirty-five-year-old girlfriend, was vegetarian, and over three years had influenced his diet. They had finally ended it the day before over a dish of hummus and chickpeas at a party given by some of her library coworkers. No doubt that's why he was feeling adrift, along with having some time to kill before he had any work to do. Plus, he sort of wished he were a nominee for the Burrison Prize. Usually, he felt no desire to be a part of the groups he served—the pharmaceutical people, the IT people, the wedding parties. Nobody here even knew he cared about writing except for Putty and Abby Bishop, and Dexter. He went back to the lobby and threw the potato in the trash behind one of the bars. He didn't disturb the woman reading the novel. Instead, he chatted with the guy reading the entertainment magazine, got the scoop on upcoming movies and TV shows, until it was time for dessert. Then he washed his hands and went back inside to help serve.

Betty Daye got up again, this time to introduce the speaker. Through small, turquoise-rimmed glasses, she read from a sheet of paper, repeating what was printed on the program, and adding that "Mr. Donny Tate is a remarkable man, a special kind of genius of survival, a man who has pulled himself up from the absolute muck of life with his great determination to redeem and remake himself, and to forge healing bonds among his splintered, wounded family. As you all know, with the help of the esteemed Tina Cockburn, his life has been translated into a powerful and bold fictionalized memoir. I am so proud and pleased to have Mr. Tate here to share his hard-earned wisdom with us." She extended her hands to him.

Tate practically leapt to the platform. He shook Betty Daye's jeweled hand and watched as she sat down. He smiled broadly, showing new teeth. He took a very deep breath before he said, "Call me Buck! My folks name me Donny. Some people wanna say Donald, but *that* not my name. Donny, after who I don't know. My friends call me Buck and I want everybody to be my friend. Buck, rhymes with…absolute muck! Ha! Luck, too. Gotta know that. *Everybody* is my friend, and *every day* is a good day."

He looked around, grinning. He seemed nervous. His eyes, which were very light for such a dark man, goldish, seemed not to know where to settle.

"All right, now what? So much for the pree-ludes. I suppose y'all wanna know how I got eighteen childrens. That what Oprah wanted to know, too. I said, how do you think, Oprah? Did y'all see that? She asked me if I knew about birth's control. When I was a boy, we didn't know hardly nothing but what we likeded and didn't like. Them little girls I was messing with then, they just took to me, that's all. And I likeded them, too. Also the grown womens, you know, then and later. They likeded my eyes, they say. I got these white eyes." He widened them. "Which by the way, I like your eyes, too, Miss Betty Daye. Like sunrise. Ha!"

Betty Daye drew back. Ray couldn't see her face, but he imagined her looking shocked and amused. Because she probably was. And she had her table to entertain.

"That how everything got started," Buck Tate said, "with me liking too much, being likeded back, and not knowing what was wrong with it. You wouldn't know anything was wrong with it, would you? But there's plenty. I went to jail. First for not paying support. Then for stealing to pay support. Other things led on from that. They tried to get me for statuary rape. Turns out, everybody wasn't none of my friend! I been shot, stabbed, beat up, lied about, operated on. I still has a bad psychotic nerve, comes and goes. Makes my leg hurt so I limp sometime. I feels good today. Oh, and I likeded mens, too, and vicey-versy.

"But I never did like childrens. I like babies, though. When I was in grade school, childrens picked at me, called me 'punk' and the like.

I got beat up. I don't like childrens 'cause you can't trust 'em. Even my grandchildrens. I used to wear vanilla flavoring on my skin, see. I likeded my hair and skin shining. Shiny long fingernails. I used to wear my pants a certain way, low on my hips so my hips could sway. I told everything to Miss Tina and she wrote it all down. But like I told Larry Kang on *The Larry Kang Show*, I have finally *almost* had enough of woman stuff now. And I don't want nothing up the butt, neither!"

When parts of the crowd laughed (Ray heard Dexter practically shriek), Tate stopped and looked baffled and surprised. But still smiling, he looked up at the ceiling, at the huge crystal chandeliers hanging in the space above the crowd like inverted twinkling trees. He chuckled. He said, "It sparkly in here."

Ray noticed Yusuf, the kid who'd helped with the podium table, standing along the far wall, poker-faced. All the serving staff, most of them black, just stood, having stopped pouring water, tea, and coffee for the speech. Yusuf held his chin high. Ray wondered what effect Tate's talk was having on him and the others.

"I'm dressed up now," Tate said, "but one time I was the dirtiest man you ever saw. I did all kinds of down-on-the-ground work. I did yard work where about I loaded up a lawnmower with rakes and clippers and pushed 'em up the roads looking for work. I might get a few dollars to eat with but my shack didn't have 'lectric and I just wore what I worked in all the time. When it were cold, I stayed in a mission for mens. Bad days, let me say. No mens or womens likes a dirty man."

Ray left the room then, astonished by Donny Tate's ignorance, his incoherence, his total lack of preparedness for such a gathering. It was embarrassing. He was furious with Betty Daye. She had invited Tate instead of Cockburn, the real writer. But both of those women had exploited Tate. One took his story, and the other stole—what? Maybe Betty Daye hadn't stolen anything. Tate didn't seem to care about his dignity; if he had any, he'd given it away. But Betty Daye had definitely used him. She knew the man would look like a fool. And she enjoyed it. And where was Cockburn now?

A voice behind him said, "How do you like old Trueblood in there?"

Ray turned to see Selma and Milla. It was Selma who had spoken, her accent pure piedmont. A few other people had come out too, headed for the bars.

"He's hard to believe," Ray said. "Not that I'm saying he's a liar."

"He's quite a character," Milla said.

Ray laughed. "Can I get you a drink?" he asked.

"Do you have beer?" asked Milla.

Selma held up two fingers. "This many," she said.

Ray went behind a bar and grabbed three iced bottles from the tub there. "I shouldn't drink here," Ray said. He had a small office he could invite them to. It was too small. "Want a tour of the kitchen?" he asked.

"Not really," Selma said. She reached in the pocket of her dress for a tissue, which she wrapped around the wet bottle. The dress was pale green. The pockets had white daisies with yellow centers embroidered along the openings, and the same pattern traced the scoop of the dress's neck.

"Sorry. You want a napkin?" he asked Milla.

She shook her head, looking at him sideways, the bottle already upturned to her lips.

Selma said. "Let's go to my car. Listen to some tunes. Drink in peace."

Ray led them out a side door and around to the front of the building. Selma's car was an old red two-door Civic. Ray sat in the back, his knees against the passenger seat where Milla sat. Selma turned on a Stevie Wonder CD. "Is this where Dexter sits?" he asked.

"We be chauffeurs," Selma said.

Milla's sleek, straight ponytail was hidden by the headrest, and Selma's crinkly hair, which spread across her back and shoulders, was held away from her face by daisy clips at the temples. Selma clinked her bottle against Milla's, and then both women turned to share the toast with Ray. "To lunch," Selma said. Ray swallowed about half his beer. Selma lit a joint with the lighter from the dashboard. The smell brought on instant nostalgia. She passed the joint to Milla, who daintily drew on it. Selma said, "The Burrison Prize is a freak show."

Ray didn't answer. He let Stevie Wonder fill the silence. He wondered what Milla knew of race subtleties in America. He knew too little about the ethnic conflicts in Bosnia, and of Germany he knew only about the WWII troubles of Jews, neither of which seemed subtle. He said, "Well, you know, it's disappointing. That's all I can say."

"Here," Milla said, giving him the joint. It was rolled with brown paper. Stevie Wonder was singing "All Is Fair in Love," and as the pot took effect, Ray's sense of nostalgia deepened. He hadn't smoked since college, when that song was soothing after his marriage ended. He'd gotten married just out of high school, and it lasted two years. Now, thinking about breaking up with his girlfriend and feeling the sad euphoria of long ago, he felt in two eras at once, like two people, even. He could see himself in the backseat of some car outside the country club where he used to work, getting high with some of his coworkers then, letting the smoke lighten his mood about his wife's unhappiness. Yet here he was now with two strange young women, trying to lighten his mood about the day before, about Buck Tate and Betty Daye, about tomorrow being empty of purpose.

He passed the joint to Selma. Suddenly he wasn't sure what race she was. He had thought she was a white woman. Not just her light skin, but the daisies as well suggested that to him. She had blue eyes, but Buck Tate had light eyes. Her nose was sort of blunt but small, and her lips were sort of full and pouty, and her hair was thick. Of course she was white, he thought, and why should he care? He didn't. But he wanted to know, and he didn't know how to ask.

Then he said, "Are you white?"

Both Selma and Milla turned around.

"Dude," Selma said. "Are you high?"

"Is Selma your real name?"

She squinted as she pulled on the joint. "No, it's Aleve," she said, exhaling. "And Milla is actually Nuprin. You got a pain and we can soothe it. Dexter tells me you got dumped last night. You want us to take the hurt away?"

"You're doing it. And it was a co-dump situation. We were a dead couple walking. Still, thanks for being medicine. Otherwise, Dexter talks too much."

"He's good gossip. That's why we like Dexter."

"I like him, too," Ray said.

"And you married young."

"Yeah. So? He told you a lot."

"That's sort of interesting. Makes you kind of romantic."

"He never said a word about you."

"We're secrets. What happened last night?"

"Nothing. I don't know. Time. Used to be I was so infatuated that I'd drive by where she lived just to see it, hoping she might be in the yard. For months she played like merely a friend, always side-stepping my little love talk. By the time she figured she could like me for real, I was pretty much over it. But I pretended I wasn't."

"Then, months later, you resented her. And she started hating you for it."

"I don't know. I guess. Ask Dexter."

"Hey, did you see Donny Tate hit on the lady who introduced him? He's *almost* given up woman stuff. Milla and I might have to meet Buck Tate ourselves."

"Are you sure you're white? Mixed, maybe?" Ray asked.

"Are we not all? It's a mixed-up shook-up world. Just ask the guy in the bathrobe. Right, Milla?"

"I'm neutral," Milla said, tight-voiced, before exhaling a conical cloud. She coughed.

"Look at me, sitting here getting stoned with race-neutral women."

"You put a word in my mouth," Milla said. She gave him back the joint, which was getting too short.

Ray squeezed in some smoke. He listened to Stevie Wonder. He shifted his weight so that he leaned against the wall behind Milla, his legs angled across the backseat. He said, "When I was a kid, I didn't know there were different kinds of white people. Then it turned out there were Jewish white people and Italian white people and Hungarians. Nowadays, there are different kinds of black people, too. First, there's all non-white people. Then, you have your Caribbean black people, your African black people, your Jewish black people, your Hispanic black people. I used to think people from India, with straight hair, were a special kind of black people, but I don't think that's what they think they are. That's when I was a kid and there'd be photos of dark, glossy-haired families on these religious brochures at church. Maybe they were Sri Lankan families. Anyway, I had a waiter once, a student who was born in Korea but was adopted and raised by a white family in Maryland. She was just starting to identify as Asian. She invited me to the Korean Student Association dinner at the university. They offered Korean food and cultural entertainment, you know, a demonstration of Korean martial arts. But then a group of boys came out and did some break dancing. Next, Korean music videos featuring a blinged-out, dyed-blond dude hip-hopping brag-rap, all swinging gold chains and sideways cap. So mixed up is definitely the thing. But leave it to Betty Daye and Buck Tate to bring back the good old pure American dichotomy and cringe."

"Wow," said Selma.

"I'm putting this out," Ray said.

"Throw it out the window."

Ray doused the joint with wet fingertips and put it in his pants pocket. "Keepsake," he said, although neither woman was looking back at him.

Milla said, "I can see the fascination with Buck Tate. I'd like to read his book. Properly organized, his story could be compelling."

"Tina Cockburn thought so," Ray said.

"I like the way he sounds," Milla continued. "Like a cross between a bulldog and melting chocolate ice cream."

"Gee," said Selma, "I want to hear that."

"Didn't you?" Milla said.

Selma said, "He sounded to me like a soft pulpy log and Juicy Fruit chewing gum."

They started laughing. Ray did too. He tried to think of what Tate sounded like to him, and it was on the tip of his tongue, but the thought of that, that phrase, plus what Milla and Selma had said, made him unable to stop laughing. Tate kind of looked like a log, and a bulldog, thick and short, and the furrows in his forehead were like chewed gum, and his words melted together, and he sounded just like he looked. Ray's stomach muscles hurt, tears blurred his vision, and the women's laughter was the same high pitch of Stevie Wonder's harmonica, which was playing "Boogie on Reggae Woman" now.

"I gots to go hear that guy again," Selma said.

"I gots to too," Milla said. They convulsed in hilarity again. They opened the car doors, let Ray out the backseat, and all three brushed ash off their clothes, laughing. Ray felt guilty for laughing at Buck. Then he realized he was probably in a paranoid haze. "He has a head like an amphitheater," Ray said.

"A coliseum," Milla said.

"A racetrack," Selma said.

"Whew!" Ray said. He was glad all he'd have to do soon was break down the room—clear the tables and gather the tablecloths—

a fairly mindless activity that being stoned should make pleasant
and light.

When they got back to the Evergreen Room they heard applause from outside the closed doors. Good, Ray thought, Donny
"Buck" Tate was done. The applause, though, was for the names of
the nominated writers, which were being recited by one of the old
men he'd seen wearing blue seersucker. He had a white handkerchief fluffed out of his jacket pocket. He had a droopy, jowly face
with a pouch of folds under his chin, pouchy eyes, and a high, wavy
white pompadour hairstyle, so that he looked like a cone of vanilla
soft-serve. Ray turned to suggest that to Selma and Milla, but they
were making their way down the side aisle toward the table they
shared with Dexter.

Soon, the man got to Dexter's name. Dexter stood, as the others
had done, and turned about and waved at the audience. Ray raised
his arm from the back, feeling proud that his buddy was in this mix.
One day, Ray thought, he too might be seated in the audience, a
feted nominee. Maybe he could write a story about a guy meeting
two beautiful women who get him high. They'd be at a party maybe,
sitting on pillows with tiny mirrors sewn into the fabric. That's what
the pillows were like at the party last night. In his story, the guy
would have just broken up with his longtime girlfriend, and would
have sworn off women for a while, but these two women would be so
much fun and so pretty that he'd want to fall in love with them both.
He'd want them, or just one, to fall for him. Yet he wouldn't know
what to say or do to manage it, because...

The ice cream man now named the winner of the Burrison Prize.
"For a book of profound emotion, compassion, and human truth,
composed of heartbreaking beauty, a book that practically emits
sparks from every page, this year's Burrison Prize goes to Imogine
Cameron, the author of *Churn*."

During the cheers and applause, a woman made her way from the middle of the room to the lectern, where she accepted the crystal bowl and a check. She stood for a moment not saying a word, just looking at the bowl. Then into the microphone she said, "Thank you," in a voice so flat and country it seemed a put-on. Her hair was long and black, curled about her shoulders like Loretta Lynn's, or some other old-fashioned country singer, and her dress was just a long drape of navy cloth. She held the bowl under one arm like a giant football. "I just want to say that this is an honor I will never forget, that I never dared to dream of. And believe me, I dream all the time." Chuckles scattered through the audience. "My book is about the kind of people I know, mountain people that always fascinated me for their courage and foolishness, their fight, you know. I couldn't have thought you'd think so much of them."

As she continued, Ray was taken by the spell of her voice. He wanted to get closer, to see better the movement of her lips, the lift of her tongue, but he didn't leave his station at the back of the room. From there, he could see that her lips were thin and pink. They produced a sound he didn't know real people made. It was beautiful and—what? Beguiling. He wanted to kiss her, as if he would taste the sound. He wanted to kiss Milla, too, who sounded, he decided, like a clarinet. And Selma, whose lips were plump and red, whose tongue was tart. He wanted them to pass their speech to him that way, kissing, kissing, kissing. He thought of Abby Bishop. He didn't want to kiss her, and shuddered to imagine it, but he did want to cast a similar spell for her. She'd tell Putty, over wine they shared in their comfortable living room, surfaces decorated with fossils and sparkly stones from Putty's geological expeditions, "You remember Ray Fielding, the waiter-slash-writer? I love that guy. I love that guy so much."

Say What?

Abby and her husband Putty had the same birthday, and on their sixty-third, they each suffered a stroke. Ray learned that much from the newspaper, a long obituary for Putty that cited his many years as a geology professor, his service to his synagogue, his marriage to Abby. First Putty fell in their kitchen and then couldn't blink his right eye, and next, after the ambulance had gotten Putty to the hospital and Abby was waiting to hear his prognosis, her vision blurred. Talking to the emergency room receptionist, she couldn't make herself understood. The receptionist called somebody and then Abby, too, was on a gurney being attached to monitors and having a light shone into her eyes. Putty had another stroke in the hospital, went comatose for three days, and died. Abbey survived. She now had a slight limp from numbness in her hip, and a disguisable weaker left arm. This much Ray learned from Abby herself, over lunch one day when she accepted his invitation to eat at a place near her house. She stopped teaching to use her disability insurance and to rehabilitate physically, and when the insurance ran out, she retired. Emeritus.

But she was apparently not forgotten. A former colleague asked her to substitute teach a fiction-writing class for one afternoon, while the colleague was on tour to promote his new novel. So she went back to work. As it happened, Ray was in that class, fulfilling a requirement toward an MFA. It was a difficult night. Ray worried about being late for the class, as he frequently was because of work, and he was surprised and unsettled to see Abby seated in front of the class.

Then the class seemed it would end early, and ugly. A student had turned in a story about a man who wakes up in the night on a soccer field and cannot remember who he is. But his ID in his wallet shows his name and address, which are unfamiliar to him. He finds his way to his building. His chest is bleeding through his shirt. He doesn't feel pain, just confusion. Turns out he's a zombie, newly minted. Abby, disappointed about the zombie turn, which seemed to be the whole point of the story—mystery solved (except for the soccer field)—suggested that the story might be better if it retained its mystery, that the zombie thing had been done to death. A few students chuckled. Maybe the question of identity was more interesting than the answer, in this case at least, etc. The student, older than most of the others except Ray, with scruff and biker boots, drawled in a squinty way, "You mean to say that if a story's about zombies it can't be good? Man, you are so full of *shit*."

"Say what?" Abby said.

"I think you got me." The student gathered his things and hustled to the door.

Abby said, "*You're* full of shit, leaving instead of listening. Is that what you said to me?"

At least the student didn't slam the door. He left it wide open, as if class were over and the other students should follow. But the others sat there, waiting for Abby to do something educational. *Observe my placid demeanor. Let that be a lesson to you.* She let the others discuss the story in the student's absence. Many of them liked the zombie surprise.

When Ray got home he was still dazed by the conflict. He imagined Abby was too. After class, he had apologized to her, offered to buy her a coffee, but she declined. He was due to submit a story next class, had wanted to talk with her about it. He imagined her getting home after six; with the passing of Daylight Savings Time, it would be nearly dark when she took her dog out for his walk.

First week of November. Fifty-six brisk degrees. Halloween decorations still haunted some houses, as they did in Ray's neighborhood. On a few front stoops, pumpkins now served the cause of Thanksgiving. She had a little pumpkin on her porch. Other houses had jumped ahead to Christmas. Lights spiraled up tree trunks and traced the eaves of certain roofs. The merging of seasons seemed to confirm Abby's sense that time was collapsing in on itself. Or was she having another stroke? She chuckled. Her eyebrows were almost as white as Santa's. As Putty's. When Putty died, five years before, her greying hair made her look regal, as he told her whenever they discussed the effects of their aging. Now, she was just old, she told herself. She was older than Putty.

The narrowing of time was so disorienting. Maybe the students could smell the rot on her. The scent of irrelevancy. In thirty-five years of teaching, she had never been cursed at by a student before. Not to her face, anyway. And she had never spoken so rudely to one, either.

On the street in front of her house, she breathed deeply and took in the sky, which retained at that moment some deep autumn blue. *Deep autumn blue*, she thought. *Or indigo. Deep Caribbean Sea. Mediterranean.* This was her second full year of retirement. She had directed two dissertations after her recovery, and had taught a summer class with the aid of a cane. Then she was out. What will you do, people invariably asked at her going away party. Write, she invariably responded. Maybe this sky would give her something, she thought. Why not?

It was the same sky outside Ray's house. He wondered if he could write about the symmetry of Abby's life with her husband's. Imperfect symmetry, it turned out. If she had died when Putty did, the coincidences of their lives would have been complete. Did Abby think about that? She must; it was her story, after all.

Bojo, a stocky tri-colored beagle, eight years old and rescued, jerked on the leash toward the other side of the street where a neighbor's garbage can was upside down, left that way since the morning trash pick-up. It wasn't Abby's neighborhood anymore, but Ray's. Yet Abby limped along. Finding nothing but scent, no biscuit or bone, Bojo tugged onward, from one side of the street to the other, zigzagging toward the road that led to the lake. "Ah, at least the lake," Abby said to her dog.

A group of boys, nine to twelve years old, gathered at the bottom of the lake road hill. The boys were always dirty whenever Abby saw them, usually in the dirt yard of the house there. They played football with a tiny ball, or tossed a flat basketball into a trashcan. Sometimes they raced each other around the lake. They called themselves the Catch Cash Kidz and the Cosmoz Goonz. Abby had seen them tagging their logos onto the planks of the pier. One, with a haughty little chest and a high little butt, had long hair parted in the middle and styled in two frayed side braids. The braids looked like dusty, chin-length turds. Now, he led a sudden chase after another boy who pedaled a bike uphill towards Abby. One of the kids shouted, "Come back here with my bike, nigga!" The rider huffed past Abby, standing on the pedals.

When Abby turned to the group again, the boys had stopped running and were breathing hard, outraged. One said, "I know! You got the registration? We can call the police!" Another kid said, "It ain't the registration; it's the model number or something. Anyway, why call the police when we can just go to his house and beat him?"

A smaller kid screamed, "He took my shoes! I'm gonna kick his ass!"

"Yo shoes over there," said the turd-braid boy.

"Where?!"

"Ova there, nigga!" He pointed into the darkness toward the yard of a house in the curve opposite the lake.

The shoeless boy hunched his body and looked. It was colder there near the water. His bare feet were on the pavement. "Where my shoes, y'all!" he yelled.

By then, Abby and Bojo were on the asphalt path that bordered the lake, heading clockwise away. The boys dashed inside their house, as if with the simultaneous and silent decision of a school of fish. The metal screen door clanked closed. The yellow porch light came on, showing a pale plastic skeleton swinging on the screen. *Oh, skeleton,* thought Abby. *You, too, are agitated.*

But the lake water was still lake water—soothing. A year before, the county had emptied the lake, scooped out and sculpted the bottom with a bulldozer, reshaped the banks, planted fresh shrubs and grass along the walking trail, and filled it again with water. The lake, which was more like a large pond, had the faint shape of a wide-bodied acoustic guitar, missing the neck. One lap was half a mile.

"Our usual, Bojo?" Abby said. Bojo ignored her, peed on a stick. The lake had been stocked with fish, turtles and frogs. Near the boat ramp, the lone blue heron that visited the lake took flight in front of Abby. It had been camouflaged by the blue darkness. It flew wide-winged and low across the water to a pine tree branch on the opposite bank. *Like an elegant shape of air,* rehearsed Abby. Ducks and geese bothered the water, which reflected dark silver light from the sky. To Abby, it was as though they swam on a large swath of silk.

She considered that description as Bojo sniffed under a picnic table on a concrete platform by the path. The dog, his nose almost always to the ground, smelled around the mesh trash bin and the iron grill littered with spent charcoal bricks. Abby looked off at the trees on the other side, the leafy tops dark against the darkening sky. *Like thumb-smudged charcoal, like charcoal smudges, like charcoal-shaped silhouettes.* Then, Bojo turned in the direction of the pier. A man emerged from the darkness there, muttering something. He had a paper bag clutched into the shape of the beer can it contained. He said, "Na-na ton shi shush." Abby said, "Right." The man said, "We can, we come, we can come here and say hello like white folks." Abby laughed a little. *Like drunk white people,* she thought, *like white people lurking in shadows.* Which wasn't unheard of. "I am white folks," she said. "Yeah," he said. "It, it's like living like white folks." Then Abby tugged Bojo back onto the path.

Abby kept thinking of ways to describe the lake with the waterfowl. *Shimmering trails on a stretch of silk. Widening ribbons drawn on the water.* It helped her to forget the disturbing class she'd just taught. She still felt strange. Insulted. Guilty.

By the time Abby and Bojo reached the next curve of the lake, the smaller, neckless end of the guitar, Abby was thinking about her neighborhood's diversity. The man with the beer, with his talk of white folks, had nudged her there. Voices drifting from far behind had also caught her attention; she couldn't make out the words, and she wondered which of her neighbors were out tonight. The neighborhood, though at some points offering a view of the city's bright skyline, was oddly rural, and mostly working-class black. But a mixture of races and incomes had lately joined the community. There was a variety of languages and dialects, too, so that sometimes what she could hear distinctly was incomprehensible. Once, she had passed two teenagers, and one said to the other, "Ah ga three hunner dahlla offa gragra." *I got three hundred dollars off of Gram-Gram,* Abby interpreted. The dialect was distinctly Southern. When she had taught full time, she warned her students against trying to write dialects, because it could make the characters seem stupid. Or from outer space. Now she wondered how she might create characters who spoke the way those teenagers spoke.

After a while, the voices behind her got closer, but no clearer. She wanted to move farther away before they caught up with her. She was a little wary of violence for some reason. Well, it was dark, and she had never been at the lake in the dark. Bojo was no guard dog. But she was also not in the mood to speak to anyone else. Bojo leaned hard into a bush that must have smelled wonderful. Abby's tug didn't faze him at all. Bojo hunkered like a bull and buried his nose.

A small square plastic bag lay next to a patch of monkey grass. Abby touched it with the toe of her sneaker. Empty. She often hoped some unhappy person might lose a full one. The neighborhood had a virulent past of crack addicts, according to some of the old-timers she'd talked with. Such bags, tossed on the side of the road, were vestiges of that era. As were shabby, vacant-eyed wanderers, and people who knocked on the door asking to clean gutters for ten dollars. Maybe that angry student was a user. Maybe meth, though, the current commodity, would be his choice. From the beginning, as Abby had entered the classroom and swept her eyes around the seminar table, that man was a rough spot. He had a stubby red beard and wore a paint-stained jean jacket. Maybe he was a true threat, the kind who shot their teachers and classmates. During the critique of the first story, about a girl who believes her daddy killed her cat, the man had said little except, "Whatever," or "I don't know, I thought it was good," squinting.

Tugging on Bojo, Abby realized she should email her colleague about the incident. If she ever got back home. Bojo took interest in a small weed, lifting his leg, and then led Abby onto the pine straw and woodchip path that formed the inner, tree-lined border to that side of the lake. It was darker there, the lights of the houses on either side partially shielded by the trees.

Before she retired, Abby often told her classes anecdotes about her community, which was then new to her. She talked about walking her dog, and described such sights as flying geese, their bellies made golden by the dawning sun. If she could tell them now about the lake at night, she'd evoke the moon on the water, planes winking high overhead, house lights quivering on the lake surface. But there was no moon now, and the student could have followed her tonight, or found out where she lived. He could be waiting among these trees where the heron had flown. Maybe he had an accomplice and was coming toward her from behind, threatening in some incomprehensible drawl.

The voices were quite near now, and one sounded female. This realization relaxed her. She could dimly make out two people coming around the neckless end of the lake. That speech was probably not the lazy slurring of the student. After she lost Putty, Abby had wanted to move to a neighborhood like this one—mixed, working class. But she was appalled at how illiterate some of these neighbors sounded and was distressed that she couldn't always understand them. It made her angry at herself. She remembered when a white woman in her former neighborhood told her about the time she substitute-taught at a black elementary school and thought they all had a speech impediment. Abby had been annoyed but amused. Now, she struggled not to feel superior to her neighbors. Sometimes she wondered if she was only feeling left out.

Of course, she could just be going deaf. She was sixty-eight years old, after all. Surprisingly. Putty used to tell her to get her ears checked. He complained about her memory, too. They had lived in a north metro suburb for twenty years, and Abby had never liked it. Too pristine, too homogeneous, too conservative. They had no children, which was always all right with them. They didn't need anyone else to love or to love them back. After thirty-four years of marriage, when he was dead and she was not, she sought something in town. Lately, though, scenes in this neighborhood made her wish Putty were alive to experience them with her, and made her miss their genteel walks in the suburbs.

Some things she could hear and understand. That morning she had gotten a call from her doctor telling her she needed to have another biopsy of her breast. Yes, she guessed that had been the start of her bad day. Something was inconclusive about last week's biopsy. Maybe this time the biopsy would show the cancer the last two had not. Later that morning, when she and Bojo were heading home during their early walk, in the much better neighborhood across the main thoroughfare, near the golf course, a man came out his front door and said, "Hey, lady, why you let your dog piss in my yard?"

Abby had expected a question like, "How old is your dog?" or "Who's walking who?" The usual. She replied, "He's just sniffing."

"I saw him," the man said. He was younger and black in a purple crewneck sweater. He drew back his shoulders and crossed his arms at his chest. His pants hung low on his hips. Bojo stood on the narrow slip of grass between the sidewalk and the artsy iron fence that traced the house's yard. That little area could hardly be called yard, Abby thought.

"He might have lifted his leg," Abby said, "but he's all peed out."

"What?"

"He's out of pee." Abby laughed to shout that from the curb.

"I *saw* him."

"I don't think so."

"So I'm lying?"

"What about the squirrels?" Abby said.

"What about them?"

Abby didn't say anything. She was trying to be rational. It was hard to take the guy seriously.

"Don't let your dog piss in my yard. I mean it."

A small dog yipped from inside the man's house. Abby imagined a caged poodle leaping about. She said, "Where does your dog pee?"

"What the hell are you talking about?"

"Where does your dog go?"

"In my *yard*," the man said, his hands on his hips now.

The man's poses annoyed Abby. She knew she should have pulled Bojo away or picked him up. Putty would have accused her of trying to get herself killed.

"I don't want *your* dog to pee in your yard," Abby said.

"What?"

"You don't want *my* dog to pee in your yard. Which he didn't. Well, *I* don't want *your* dog to pee in your yard," Abby repeated. "Let him pee somewhere else."

"You old crazy bitch," the man said. "Get the hell away from here before I come down there."

Abby felt scared and invigorated by the exchange. Sure, she was old, but she was a crazy bitch. *How's that, Putty?*

Now, looking behind her, she could see the people doing the talking. They were the grandparents of the immigrant Asian family that lived in the large brick house at the top of the lake road. She'd never learned their exact ethnicity, and didn't know what language they spoke to each other. Whatever it was, it was fast. By their gesturing hands and overlapping chatter, Abby had the sense that they were arguing. Bojo decided then to squat and shit, as they passed by.

"Hello," said Abby.

"Hi," they said. Or "Hai."

After stooping to bag the shit, Abby hurried Bojo along, pulling on the leash. She no longer feared that the student would attack her at the lake, or that crack hounds were on her heels. *Crack Hounds*, she thought. *A novel.* She got back on the road, treaded up the hill, and then was back on her street. She was ready to email her colleague and have some dinner, watch TV, write down her memories of the day. But probably drink something and go to sleep. There was still about a quarter mile to go, and more unturned trash cans, fallen leaves, and blades of grass for Bojo to inspect. They stopped near a house where the current occupants, a woman and her young son, bred pit bulls. Orange holiday candles were lit in the front windows. Cages for the dogs were in the back, mostly shielded by a slat fence. The woman stood at her curb talking to another woman and a preteen girl. Maybe they were negotiating on a puppy. Yesterday, the thirteen-year-old son had approached Abby cradling a brown frightened-looking dog in his arms. He had asked if Abby wanted to buy it. His mother, light-skinned with wild hair, wearing a man's trench coat, said to the other woman, "We keep them fenced in and caged most of the time. They need exercise. Any barking the dogs do is incidental." She had, Abby noticed, clear speech.

The visiting woman said, "Motherfuck incidental. Them goddamn dogs needs to go."

"They're not dangerous in any way, you know. They're just dogs."

"Motherfuck a dog. They loud, and they scares my girl. She's a scary child and pits kill. You got a chance now before I calls the police."

The woman in the trench coat said, "Lady, call who you got to."

Bojo sniffed about the woman's mailbox, not ten feet from where she stood. He was intent on something in the grass there, under a streetlight, but his long floppy ears hid what it was. Abby didn't want to be cursed at again today. She dragged Bojo away, offended by the talk for the dog's sake.

She looked ahead as a car approached. Its headlights showed a man in a white T-shirt walking toward her. From the sideways angle of his cap and the bear-like shuffle of his walk, Abby recognized him as one of the men who sometimes milled outside at the drink house. The man had a beautiful singing voice, which accompanied the R&B

CDs they played when they gathered outside with their cups. Abby watched him lope across the yard of the house and climb the stairs. When the door opened, the man shouted, "Don't you ever disrespect me again."

"I do respect you," said the man who had opened the door. "I respect you a lot."

"You disrespect me again and it will be the last thing you ever do. You hear me?"

"I respect you. I do."

"The last thing, buddy, I'm telling you. You'll be in a goddamn body bag."

Wow, Abby thought. She couldn't figure out why there was so much enmity in the air. Maybe *she* was spreading it. Maybe she had caught something like an anger infection from the student, or from that guy in the purple sweater this morning, and was spreading it through her community just by walking her dog. Or was it a citywide phenomenon, happening on every street, making families playing Scrabble toss the board and choke each other?

Several yards farther was the house where another white family lived, not one of the young families, but, from all appearances, people who had been there for decades. It was a narrow brick house with a clutter of junk on the side screened porch. A young man lived there with his parents, an old plump woman who wore sack-like dresses of faded flower prints and a skinny old man who wore jeans and flannel plaid shirts. The son had a dented and rusted vintage truck. It was parked on the street, as usual. Their old gray Cadillac was on the grass-and-dirt lawn and the old man and woman sat inside it with the doors open, the interior lights on. *Illuminating them,* Abby considered. The son stood at the hood of the car. He said, "I cain't find no motor to fit it. I done told you that!" His protesting voice was twangy and high-pitched. In warm weather he usually wore a tank top to cover his big belly, and always he wore his hair in a long, graying mullet, the temples sheared close. Tonight, he had an unbuttoned flannel shirt over the tank. Abby raised her hand in greeting, but nobody looked her way. Then, Bojo suddenly turned left to go down another street. This change of route was out of the norm, but Abby allowed it. They could circle the block and come out again at her street, nearer her house.

This stretch of the walk was even darker than the dark side of the lake. There were no streetlights, few lighted porches because too many of the houses were abandoned, and no lake to reflect any lights from the windows of the occupied houses. This was the trouble with standard time. It meant Abby would have to walk her dog in the dark until March. She'd have to get a light-colored jacket and maybe a reflective leash to keep from getting hit by a car, as there were no sidewalks, either.

When a car did come along, Abby saw the form of another man up ahead, staggering away. The man was listing, dressed in dark clothing, smoking something. He proceeded slowly, but if Bojo were to sniff and piss at every odd moment, they might not overtake him before they reached the next street and headed home, avoiding another drunk or irritated neighbor. Bojo behaved as expected, poking his nose into a pile of discarded couch pillows and a broken headboard that the garbage men had not removed. But the man suddenly stopped, pulled on his smoke, and weaved in the middle of the street. When Abby and Bojo got near, Bojo angled his nose toward the man. The man's skin seemed unnaturally dull and dark, as if from some transformative illness, and his eyes in the glow of the cigarette seemed as red as the burning tip. Smoke swathed his head, and Abby imagined for a moment that he was the source of all the discontent, or maybe the disoriented zombie from her student's story sprung into reality, unsure of where he was going or of where he was. With the hand that held the cigarette, he reached to touch Bojo's head, and Abby flinched at the thought of Bojo being burned, of his having to breathe the acrid smoke. Bojo looked up at the man, and the man seemed to smile, making a grumbling sound. "Good bunny," it sounded like.

"It's a dog," Abby said uncertainly.

Then she realized she'd wandered into a trap. She had walked into her own zombie story. She was already on borrowed time, a cliché she often told herself. She should have died when Putty died. That's when all the charm went away. Sometimes in bed she even prayed to die, and Bojo would come to the side and sniff her. But if she had cancer, she possibly was the walking dead. Well, she was in the right place, he guessed. The place was filled with the walking lifeless. Drunks, addicts, the discontent.

A siren wailed in the distance. Her neighbors were still yelling. At her driveway, Abby stopped to check her mailbox. There was something, but it was too dark to see what. The front of her house was dark, too. Either she had not remembered to turn on her porch light, or the bulb had blown again. "Which?" she asked Bojo.

Yes, this was her house. That was her car in the driveway. But she couldn't see the pumpkin on the porch. The man with the mullet was still arguing with his parents in the Cadillac. The shouts were louder, and Abby imagined the horrified looks on all their angry faces, like the expression of the boy whose bike was taken, and the boy who had lost his shoes. Abby was sure of what the man was screaming. "Stop saying that! Just stop saying that! I wish you would damn it stop saying that!"

Acknowledgments

I am very grateful to Heather Russel, Kathleen Ochshorn, Josh Russell, Michelle Dotter, Kelly Craigmile, Bennie O. Holman, The Corporation of Yaddo, and Georgia State University for their support for this book, and to the editors of the following journals and magazine for publishing versions of these stories. "Cannon" and "Sunday," *Tampa Review*; "Gifted" and "The Naked Eye," *Oxford American*; "Second Fire," *Third Coast*; "Wave," *Image*; "Vacation," MississippiReview.Com; "Luau," *Mississippi Review*; "Say What?" *Chattahoochee Review*; "The Burrision Prize," *Terminus*.